AS SUYI DAVIES OKUNGBOWA

David Mogo, Godhunter
Son of the Storm

AS SUYI DAVIES

Minecraft: The Haven Trials

MINECRAFT™

THE HAVEN TRIALS

MINECRAFT™

THE HAVEN TRIALS

SUYI DAVIES

NEW YORK

Copyright © 2021 Mojang AB. All Rights Reserved.
Minecraft, the Minecraft logo, and the Mojang Studios logo
are trademarks of the Microsoft group of companies.

Published in the United States by Del Rey, an imprint of
Random House, a division of Penguin Random House LLC, New York.

DEL REY is a registered trademark and the CIRCLE colophon
is a trademark of Penguin Random House LLC.

Published in the United Kingdom by Del Rey UK,
an imprint of Cornerstone,
a division of Penguin Random House UK.

Hardback ISBN 978-0-593-35575-6
International ISBN 978-0-593-35904-4
Ebook ISBN 978-0-593-35576-3

Endpapers: M. S. Corley

Printed in the United States of America on acid-free paper

randomhousebooks.com

2 4 6 8 9 7 5 3 1

First US Edition

Book design by Elizabeth A. D. Eno

For the friends we find on life's most treacherous journeys,
and the lessons they teach us along the way

PART ONE

THE
SUDDEN
MOVE

CHAPTER ONE

WE ARE MOVING.

The text message had arrived at night, at exactly 12:01 A.M. Reading it now on the blinking family tablet, Cecelia wondered why Therese had waited until she was asleep before sending it. Cece loved and adored her best friend, and if there was anything she thought she knew about Therese, it was this: surely Therese would never abandon her.

And yet, there it was, a single line packed with the possibility of disappointment: *We are moving.*

Cece jumped out of bed and ran the whole way to her parents' bedroom.

"They're moving, they're moving!" She barged through the door.

It was a Saturday, so Iya and Baba were still in bed late, each in their pajamas. They jumped, startled.

"Ei, ei," Baba, who was also "Daddy" sometimes but insisted Cece refer to her parents using the traditional Yoruba terms, said. "Why all this shouting this morning?"

"And what did we say about knocking before entering?" Iya, who was also "Mummy," asked.

"Yes, yes, okay, scold me later," Cece said. "But we must go now."

"Because?" Baba inquired.

"Because Reesa and her family are moving and I won't be able to say goodbye if we don't leave *right now!*"

It took quite a bit of prodding for them to boot up like slow computers and get up to speed. As they had decided it was too early to let her out alone, Cece managed to persuade them to come with. She literally had to drag them out of the house and into the cold morning, both still in their bathrobes. Cece herself was in her bathroom slippers, but who cared? Therese was *leaving.* All Cece could think about was getting there before it was too late.

Gemshore Estate, their neighborhood in the island part of Lagos, was just waking up as well. The streets were empty but for the Saturday street sweepers. The *swish swish* of their brooms and the call of early birds were the only sounds for miles. Cece's parents paused to greet one of the sweepers, smiling and saying È kàáró oh! in a singsong voice. The sweeper himself chirped a sugar-sweet *Good morning!* Cece's way. But Cece was already out of earshot, abandoning her parents behind and running for Therese's.

The family home of the Njingas, Therese's parents, was only six houses down from Cecelia's, but around the bend. Her parents finished their greetings and caught up as she turned the corner. Cece expected to see moving trucks and a lot of activity come into view as they neared the Njinga house. Instead, misty silence greeted them at the detached duplex. The garage door was rolled down, there was no car parked in the compound, and all the windows were shut.

There was no one there.

"What is happening? Where are they?" Cece turned to her parents, a plea in her eyes. "Where is Therese?"

"Oh, honey," Iya said, and patted Cece's shoulder. "I think we may be too late."

Back home, Cece sat at the dining table and tried to process what had just happened. *How could Reesa do that?* she thought. How could her one and only friend in the world just move away without telling her or giving her the opportunity to say goodbye?

While Baba spoke on the phone, trying to reach Mr. Njinga for an explanation of the family's sudden disappearance, Iya made Cece her favorite beverage: hot chocolate with honey and marshmallows. Or, her favorite beverage when she was, like, five—not that Iya could be bothered to remember she was not five anymore. Cece *was* in need of warmth, though, and decided, *Hot chocolate is fine, I guess.* However, when it did come, she was too downbeat to drink any of it, and just let it sit there, getting cold.

We were supposed to start Gemshore Secondary together on Monday. Cece picked at her fingers, nervous just at the thought. *How am I supposed to start secondary school all on my own?*

While her mother rummaged around trying to make breakfast, Baba finished his phone call.

"They're already at the airport," he announced after hanging up. "They're getting ready to board. He says they're moving to a place called Scottsdale. It's in the USA."

"Why didn't she tell me it would happen so fast?" Cece asked, to no one in particular. "Why did she wait until last night?"

"Well, Mr. Njinga says it was quite sudden and there was little time to plan. None of his children even knew they were moving this quickly—not Therese, not her brothers."

"But still . . ."

"Honey dearest," Iya said. "I know it feels horrible to lose your best friend, but I'm sure she would have told you if she could. Don't worry—once they land, you can speak to her on your Baba's phone."

Cece ate the rest of her breakfast in uncharacteristic silence. Midway through her meal of wheat bread with mayo and sausages, the tablet chimed again. Iya picked it up, put on her glasses, and squinted at it.

"I think it's your friend," she said, and passed the iPad to Cece.

I'm sorry I didn't tell you, the message from Therese read. *It was very . . . fast.*

Cece put down the tablet and finished her breakfast. Once done, she went to the den, the only other room with a TV besides the living room, where her video gaming console was hooked up. She pulled a beanbag chair across, settled into the plush foam in front of the TV, booted up the unit, slipped on her headphones, and picked up her controller.

After breakfast on weekends was often housekeeping time, then homework time, then screen time, which could be a game or TV. But the housekeeper had come early the day before— a public holiday—and helped Cece with folding her clothes and arranging her books and putting her socks in the washer. Today being a weekend following a public holiday also meant she had done her homework the day before. Now, all she had was free time to do whatever she wished with.

But only as the game world wrapped around her did she remember that with Therese gone, she had no one to play Minecraft with.

I spawn right at the heart of Silver Oaks Park.

That is what Reesa and I named this Realm. There is no silver here, really, or oak trees. It was just the name we could come up with the first time we learned how to craft a sign out of wood planks and a stick. We stuck the sign in the ground, wrote in the letters, and named it our own private corner of the big world of Minecraft.

What I'm calling the "heart" is really the house Reesa and I built three years ago at what is now the center of Silver Oaks. Three years ago, I was goofing around on a public server for players around the estate, hiding from mobs in a tiny wooden shack. But instead of a zombie, *i_am_therese* spawned where I was, peered into my hiding spot, and asked if she could come hide with me.

She explained to me that there were Peaceful Realms where monsters didn't exist. Just things like polar bears and iron golems, which don't bother you if you don't bother them. She told me she had a private Realm set to Peaceful, and invited me. I later found out that her father was paying to host this Realm for her for the same reason I was trying not to play Minecraft elsewhere. And that was to avoid venturing into the big bad world of public servers on the internet.

We became friends that night, and have been ever since. She told me her name was really Teresa, but that her grandparents, who were originally from Congo-Brazzaville, opted to call her Thérèse, after a once-popular French princess where they grew up. It had stuck, and everyone called her Therese now. But she asked that I call her Reesa for short. It was what she let only her best friends call her.

I walk through the house we built together. It is no longer a small hiding spot, but now a mansion with more rooms than we can manage. We have crafted beds, books, bookshelves, carpets, banners, fences, gates. We have a small basement we built with cobblestone where we keep most of our booty. Our large living room has tall, floor-to-ceiling, stained glass windows. We crafted a few framed paintings and placed them around the house.

But it is not only the mansion at Silver Oaks that is our stamp on the world. As I look over the balcony of the first floor of our house, I can see all the farms we have created. Wheat, beetroot, cocoa beans, melon, pumpkin, mushrooms, sugarcane: all growing around us. There is even a barn where we keep sheep whenever we have the time to tend to them.

Even some things that we once did that are no longer here I remember now just by looking. Like that one time we decorated for the new year holidays. Or the time we made eggs and hid them and then tried to do an Easter egg hunt thing. I hid mine high up in a tree, and Therese tried to climb it once she had figured it out, but just kept falling. The memory comes to me now and I can't help laughing.

Silver Oaks Park is our paradise. Or *was*. Because for the first time in the existence of Silver Oaks, it is not friendly and fun chatter that greets my arrival, but a lonely silence. And staring back at me, everywhere I look, is the realization that one thing about this place that might not change for a long time is this: *i_am_therese is offline.*

CHAPTER TWO

MONDAY WAS GOING TO BE a drag, and Cece knew it.

The day began with a gray and grumpy sky that matched Cece's foul mood. Breakfast tasted like the sadness that filled her chest. And though it didn't rain as Iya drove her to her first day of secondary school, the wind was whooshing past the car and making a sound like a TV without a working channel.

When their car pulled up at the school parking lot, Iya reached out and kissed Cece's forehead.

"I know you're feeling down, dearest," she said. "But you're only ten years old—"

"Ten and a half," Cece said.

"Okay, okay, ten and a half," Iya said. "Still, I want you to remember that you have a whole life ahead of you. I understand that you have lost contact with Therese, and that she has been your best friend throughout primary school." Iya pointed to the school building before them. "But maybe you should think of this as an opportunity to make new friends. You are nice, sweet, and funny. I'm sure there are many children in that building right now who can't wait to meet you and become your friend."

With that, Iya bid her goodbye and drove off. Cece stood on the pavement, bag in hand, and stared up at the front façade of Gemshore Private Secondary School.

It wasn't entirely new *new*, the school. They had ridden past it many times, because it was located within the estate, and was the sister secondary school to Gemshore Primary, which Cece had attended until now. Half the new students at the school would simply be her former classmates from primary school, mixed with some new ones from outside the estate. Still, this was only the second time Cece would be entering the building, the other being when she and Iya had come here for registration months ago.

And this was the first time she would be entering the building *alone*.

"Therese, you mad girl," Cece muttered under her breath. "We would have been doing this together. I guess I'll have to do it alone now."

The walk to assembly was short and uneventful. The directions were clear at the main gate: *All new students, follow the green arrows to the assembly*, a conspicuous sign had read. Cece followed the arrows, milling among many new students in shiny new uniforms just like hers.

She had seen many films about first days of school, and read books about them, too. And in those stories, the first day of school never went well. She half-expected some bully or troublemaker to bump into her and then size her up and pronounce her a weirdo or nerd. Those stories had taught her that unless someone was the coolest new kid in school, they were always quickly put in their place.

For her, that place was closer to the bottom of the cool-kid lad-der than she would have liked. She didn't have any special skills or traits she could think of that would make people like her—her interests were reading fantasy books and playing Minecraft. Not even the hard Minecraft—just simple, fun, goofing-around Mine-craft.

Therese was supposed to be here. Together, they were sup-posed to look out for each other, elevate each other, protect each other. Cece had heard stories—gossip from classmates back at Gemshore Primary—that senior students at Gemshore Second-ary were mean. She'd heard they would whistle at a junior student and send them off on impossible errands, like, *Fill up this basket with water, using only a teaspoon.*

However, Cece soon found that real life was unlike the mov-ies. There was no bully, no put-down, no remarkable event. Ev-eryone pretty much ignored her and the other new students. Even those whose faces she recognized from around the estate—new and old students alike— pretended not to know one another.

The assembly was quick and uneventful, too: national an-them, prayer, and a few announcements. Then the new students were shepherded into a corner while everyone else left. Various teachers approached and called lists of names, after which the students went with them to their new classes. Finally, a tall man in a waistcoat said, "Cecelia Alao," and Cece raised her hand in response, then followed him alongside a bunch of other stu-dents.

Next were desk assignments. Cece's was smack in the middle of her home classroom. She heaved a sigh of relief. A seat in the middle of class was the kind of invisible she liked: not too con-spicuous, but not too hidden, either. Plus, it helped that she didn't have to contend with the territorial markers that came with class seating.

Cece thought of class seating territories the same way she thought about Minecraft mobs. There were four zones in class seating: the *windowers* sat in the window rows on either side of class; the *teacher's pets* sat in the front rows; the *backbenchers* sat at the very rear of class; and the invisible folks like her in the middle were so invisible they had no name. Belonging to a faction came with certain labels and reputations—some good, some not so great—but they also came with privileges.

Cece thought of the teacher's pets, for instance, as villagers protected by an iron golem. You annoyed this faction at your own peril, because the minute they reported you to a teacher, for any reason whatsoever, you were in hot soup. Even senior students knew to avoid teacher's pets.

Windowers were like neutral mobs: they left you alone as long as you did the same with them. But they were also too unpredictable to be trusted. They were the wolves of the class, in that they came in all shapes and sizes and forms, and would cause trouble only if they were accosted or felt they'd been treated wrongly. Most times, though, they offered protection to those under attack by going on the offense themselves.

The backbenchers were the hostile mobs: the creepers, zombies, skeletons, Endermen. They sniffed out trouble and started something every opportunity they got. And since the teacher's pets were out of reach, they were always seeking out victims in windowers and invisibles who weren't invisible enough.

Cece knew that there were people who didn't really conform to the behaviors and patterns of the areas they sat in. But groups possessed a certain enchantment, and Cece had observed that belonging to one reputed to be full of mean people turned even the most happy-go-lucky kids mean. Which was why she had avoided making new friends herself, and had so far limited her friendship connections to Therese.

That gamble had now backfired, of course. Therese was gone, and Cece was back to being alone. Perhaps now was a good time to rethink that strategy.

Cece observed the shiny new uniforms around her, everyone setting up their desks. A boy displayed his cool new notebooks up near the front, stacking and arranging them neatly and beaming, likely hoping someone would come by and compliment them. A girl with a very intricate plait that had colored beads woven into them was smiling at everyone who went by her, greeting them with a cheery *Good morning!*

Everyone's already trying to make friends, thought Cece. *Maybe I should stop moping about and try.*

So, when the next new girl went by, Cece said hi.

The girl was only slightly taller than Cece, and just as skinny. She had tight little eyes that she squinted even further as she looked Cece over and tried to determine if she should respond or not.

"Cool bag you have there," Cece said, even though she had not taken a good look at it. And now that she did, she saw that it was quite frayed, and looked like a hand-me-down. The girl was likely from outside of the estate—the kids who lived on the estate would never be caught dead with that bag. That had to be why the girl didn't look familiar.

The girl eyed her backpack, then looked over at Cece's.

"What's that?" she asked, pointing at the sticker of a creeper's face Cece had stuck on her bag.

"Oh, that's a creeper," Cece said. The girl's face did not register recognition. "From Minecraft, the video game? Building blocks and villagers?" When the girl shook her head, Cece added, "Well, I can tell you about it. My friend, Reesa—she's moved away now—we have matching stickers, and we used to—"

"Oh, I don't care," the girl said, cutting in. "I wasn't saying I don't know what Minecraft is. I just don't care. Nobody does."

With that, she brushed past and went to her new seat—at the very rear of the class.

A *backbencher*, Cece thought, biting her lip to absorb the hurt of the girl's harsh words. *That's what you get for moving too close to a creeper, Cece. It explodes in your face.*

Cece slid her bag into her desk. A moment later, she retrieved it, tore the sticker off, and threw it in the trash can.

Iya had been wrong. This making-new-friends business was going to be much, much harder than she thought.

CHAPTER THREE

"FIRST DAY OF SECONDARY SCHOOL, eh, dearest?" Iya said on the ride home. "How was it? Feel like a big girl yet?"

"It was rubbish," Cece said, moving the passenger seat back so that she was almost lying flat on the backseat. "Complete rubbish. And I don't feel anything—I just want to go home and sleep."

"Ah-ah now, don't be so negative," Iya said. "Okay, tell me at least one good thing that happened today."

Cece thought back to the day. After that incident with the backbencher girl and the sticker, she had barely spoken to anyone else. A teacher or two came by, but they only did their duty and left. During break time, she had eaten her lunch alone in silence, seated in a corner of the food court. In fairness, many of the other new students had seemed to be having the same experience. She saw others scattered around the food court like her, probably tetchy about making the first move to turn their isolation into friendship. Having already been bit, Cece resisted the urge. Instead, she ended up thinking a lot about Therese, and how she needed to speak with her *real* friend as soon as possible.

"Nothing," Cece said. "Nothing good happened." She leaned forward. "Has Therese called yet?"

Iya shook her head and gave a wry smile. Cece slumped back into her seat, discontent.

"It can take a while to settle, these things," Iya said. "Maybe you can plan one of your sleepover-type things? Only it'll be virtual—you can talk over the phone or video call on the tablet. You can even do it while in your pajamas, like a real sleepover."

Cece grunted, though the idea didn't sound half-bad. She filed it away for future use.

Once they arrived home and Cece had changed, she took Iya up on her offer and sent a message to the number saved on the family tablet as "Mr. Njinga."

How far? she typed. *Are you settled in yet? First day at Gemshore Sec was trash. I miss yoouuu!* She paused for a moment, thinking of a way not to sound too desperate. *Iya says I should ask if we can do a "phone sleepover." Like, in our pajamas and on video chat. So stupid, I know. What do you think?*

She left the tablet and went to do some house chores, mostly changing her bedsheets and folding some laundry. When she was done and returned to the tablet, there was a response from Therese: one simple word.

Sure.

Cece should have known that the first sign things were not going to go so well was the WiFi connection acting up five minutes before the sleepover.

There she was, all dressed up in her pajamas and excited. Iya and Baba had let her have the tablet in her room, all alone, something they seldom did. Not that she would need it for long, anyway—the plan was that after she caught up with Therese, they would play a bit of Minecraft together, hang out at the ole sanctuary for as long as they could. It had been weeks since they last did that, and Cece ached for it.

"Babaaa!" Seated cross-legged on the rug in her room, Cece chucked her head out the door and peeked down the corridor. "Internet is not working!"

"Have you turned it off and on again?"

Cece rolled her eyes. That was Baba's solution to everything—turn it off and on again.

"I've done that a thousand times," she said.

"Well, technically, you cannot have done it a thousand times, because—" Her father appeared in the hallway in his pajamas, took one look at her, and shook his head. "Just . . . gimme."

He took the tablet and tapped it a number of times, then handed it back to her. "There."

It was already a few minutes past the agreed hour before Therese picked up, after Cece had called three times.

"Cece!" Therese said as soon as she came on the screen.

"Reesa!" Cece couldn't contain herself. "Aaah!"

"Ohmygosh, I wish I could, like, hug you right now," Therese said. "You look so good!"

"And you look good, too!" Cece said, then stopped. "Wait, why are you not in your pajamas?"

Not only was Therese not in her pajamas, she was *outside*. Behind her, there were large mountains sticking into the sky, and palm trees. The sun shone brightly on her face.

Therese laughed. "I can't be in my pajamas, silly. It's like after-noon here."

"Oh, wow. Is that the time-difference thing my parents are al-ways talking about? How many hours is it?"

"Eight—behind you," Therese said. "So whatever your time is, you remove eight hours from it, and that's the time we're at."

"Wow." Cece leaned into the screen. "And you look like you're on holiday!"

Therese did, indeed, look like she was on vacation. She had a pair of sunglasses tucked into her hair, which she had now braided long, something her parents would never allow her to do back in Lagos. And even if they did, the school wouldn't—Gemshore Secondary accepted only all-back cornrows in short plaits or a low haircut. Therese was also wearing lip gloss—another thing her parents would never let her do back in the estate. Her skin seemed to be glowing, and for a moment, Cece wondered if the sun in Scottsdale was different from the sun in Lagos. Her own skin would never glow like that, no matter how she tilted the camera for selfies.

This should have been Cece's second sign of things to come.

"Oh, it's not vacation, it's hard work," she said. "Moving into a new house, arranging my room all over again—ugh. Plus, I have to start a new school and everything. It's not great."

"Yeah, me, too," Cece said. "Today was the first day of Gem-shore Sec."

"Ooh, how did it go?"

"It suuucked! I just kept wishing you were here."

Therese giggled. "Yeah, I can guess. Did you make any friends yet?"

"I tried. The girl was mean."

"Eeya, sorry," Therese said. "I'm trying here, too."

"Ooh, nice, is it working?"

"Somehow, somehow." Therese looked off to the side of the camera. "It's not that bad."

"That's so nice," Cece said. "I can't wait to tell you everything—first day of school, estate gossip, the new playlists I've made. Also, all the new stuff I've added to Silver Oaks—I'll show you when we play. So many things have happened since you left!"

"Oh, right," Therese said. "About that. I kinda have to go."

"Wait, what?"

"I have a thing," Therese said, looking off-camera again. "I—"

"Reesa?"

"I'm so sorry, Cece—can we talk later?" She was looking fully out of the camera now, her voice fading away with her increasing distance from the phone mic. "I'm not sure the sleepover can happen because of this time zone-difference thing, but . . . we can make something happen."

Cece opened her mouth to ask how and when, but the call had already ended.

What's so silvery about Silver Oaks Park again?

As I spawn back into our Realm, this is the thought that welcomes me. It's night in the world, just as it's night outside of it. I stand there, looking around, watching the gray notification above me that says i_am_therese is offline.

"Offline in here, offline out there, offline everywhere," I say out loud to myself.

A pixelated cow nearby grunts in response.

I decide I will not mope about it this time, and will instead try to play for real and get a thing or two done. If I remember correctly, both our coal supplies were running low the last time Reesa and I were here together, and some of the new portions of the mansion we just built are not yet lit. Now that it's night, it would be a good time to gather some coal and make a few more torches for those places.

I make my way toward the mountain closest to our base, which we nicknamed "coal mountain" because it was the first reliable source of mineral veins we found while trying to build up our base.

I've gone quite far before everything becomes super dark, so dark I can no longer see my own hands, and I remember I did not take a torch for myself. It's too dark to find my way back alone like this, so I decide to craft a torch instead.

I still have some wood planks from the last time I mined trees. I make sticks and, using the last blob of coal I have left, I craft four torches. Then I break the crafting table back down, and I am soon back on my way.

I pass by a wolf. It does not even acknowledge me.

The journey to the mountain is short. Most of the coal is gone—Therese and I have mined all of the visible mineral veins. We even mined down to the bedrock in some spots, and found some diamonds once. There are only a few spots left to try for veins, and they don't really offer any even after I hack and hack. Soon, I'm too far away from the torches, and I have to go back up and get them, place them in new locations, and continue the digging process.

Minecraft suddenly feels like hard work. Too much hard work.

I keep digging in random spots, and when I continue to find no sign of coal, I decide I'm done. But I've dug too far inside, and to climb out—and then walk the whole way back—is a hassle.

So I open my command bar and type in the command I need to respawn me at base:

[/kill @cece_lao]

You Died, my screen announces over a reddish tint, and then I'm suddenly back at base, automatically respawned.

The unlit spots are still there, though night is almost over and it looks like dawn is coming. I decide to redistribute the torches we have anyway, spread the light out. Then I remember I left the torch I made back at the mountain. I punch at a block in frustration, and after a few punches, it shatters and drops. I punch another, then another, and soon I'm punching everything in sight. I go into the basement where we've left our tools, take up a pickaxe, and hack at everything I see on my way back up to the level. It is the first time I've felt useful here since Therese left, and I keep going, leaving a pattern of destruction in my wake.

Soon, I'm at the sign that says *Silver Oaks Park.*

What's so silvery about Silver Oaks Park again?

Reesa was. Without her, this Realm, this park, all of this world — it's all nothing. As majestic and well-built as our base is, it is just a quiet and lonely place now. And as much as I want to stay here, I don't know if I can stay in this world without her.

If she can't wait long enough to go play with her new friends to log on to the world we spent so many of our best days building, then I'm not waiting for her, either.

I raise the pickaxe and hack at the sign until it is destroyed.

CHAPTER FOUR

CECE WOKE UP HORRIFIED THE next morning. The events of the night before came back to her like a bad dream. What exactly had possessed her? Had that truly been her, hacking and hacking and hacking at everything she and Therese had built? She tried to think about how far she had gone in her destructive path, but she just couldn't remember. Had she stopped and suddenly returned to her senses? Or had she continued to hack at the only thing she and Therese had left of each other, until there was nothing left?

"Morning, dearest," Iya said once Cece had showered and dressed for school. She bid her mother good morning, but was preoccupied by the night before. She headed straight to the console to check, but Iya stopped her.

"Ah, ah," her mother said. "You only have time for breakfast, so you can't do games." She pointed at the food she was setting up for Cece. "Table, now."

So Cece ate, still wondering. When it was time to leave for school, and Iya wasn't looking, she slipped the family tablet into her bag. She chose to sit in the back of the car this time, where Iya couldn't easily see her. As her mother fought through estate rush-hour traffic, Cece hunkered down in her seat, pulled open Minecraft, and clicked Play. Then she navigated to Silver Oaks under the Friends tab and tapped.

Nothing happened.

She frowned and tapped it again, then peered closer at the screen. Nothing. She went up to the Realms tab that read **Therese's Gaming Realm—i_am_therese (owner)**. At the side of the bar, there should have been a green button that told her the Realm was alive and kicking. But instead, she saw a grayed-out button.

"Weird," she pondered aloud, tapping and tapping, hoping something would happen. No dice. Had she done something even more stupid—like mistakenly delete the Realm? Or worse—had she and Therese been so caught up with moving and starting new schools that they both missed some sort of warning message that the Realm was going to expire?

Cece threw down the tablet, horrified anew. Did an expired Realm mean everything—*everything*—was gone?

She had thought yesterday's events were a bad dream. Today was proving to her that it was more than that: it was a nightmare.

Cece spent most of first through fourth periods trying to piece together what had happened. Rather than pay attention to the English and social studies teachers, she pondered if it was her actions that had led to the Realm being expired. Or worse, deleted. *"Expired" isn't the same as "deleted,"* she kept telling herself, but remained unsure. She had never understood the goings-on behind the private shared Realm she and Therese had played in all this time, but she knew that Mr. Njinga paid the subscriptions that allowed them to continue to do so. Had that been revoked for some reason?

As break time arrived and Cece headed out to the food court, her mind ran into even wilder places. Maybe Therese had opened the game and seen Cece's destruction and therefore asked her father to cancel the subscription? Or, worse yet, had canceled it herself? These thoughts ping-ponged in Cece's brain so nonstop that she wound up arriving later than she'd wanted to the food court's only canteen.

Once she arrived, the canteen was full and the line was long. The selling lady today was slow and, with a mass of clamoring students to attend to, not in the best of moods, either. The senior students had a separate break time to avoid bullying, so it was just her mates and the older juniors rallying about the food court. Iya had been in a hurry today and did not prepare packed snacks, and so she'd given Cece money to get herself some food.

When Cece had first seen the crowd, her interest had waned. But she decided now to wait them out. She sat in a corner of the food court, continuing to ponder the future of Silver Oaks Park, and what might have become of the tiny thread of friendship she had left with Therese.

Soon, someone tapped on her shoulder. She turned around to see a boy from her class—the same one who had sat in front with his notebooks arranged on the first day—staring back at her. He was shorter than he'd initially seemed, and Cece was surprised to realize she'd be taller than he was if she stood up. He was, however, a tad chubbier than her slim self, and had hair that, though short, was unnaturally frizzy. A smile was plastered on his face, chirpy and expectant, as if he just knew that good things would always come his way.

"Hi," he said.

"Hi," Cece said back, confused. *Why is he here? Surely he couldn't just be coming by to, like, chat with her?*

"I found this in the trash," he said, passing a piece of crumpled paper to her. Cece took it. It was the sticker of the creeper she had tossed away on the first day of school.

"I wanted to give it to you all this time but . . ." He trailed off.

"Oh," Cece said. "Um . . . thanks?"

"Sorry you had to throw it away in the first place," he said. "I saw what happened . . . with Ofure."

"Ofure?"

"The girl with the plaits who sits at the back of class? Who made fun of your sticker?"

"Oh, that's her name?"

"Yeah. And she sucks—not just with you, don't worry. She sucks like that with everyone."

"Oh."

"Yeah." He paused again. "I'm Joachim."

"Hmm," Cece said, still lost in her own thoughts.

"And you are?"

"Me? Cece. Short for Cecelia."

"Cecelia." He nodded, wringing his hands, seemingly deciding whether to ask a question or not. He finally went with asking.

"Are you, like, going to buy something for lunch or . . . ?"

"I want to," Cece said. "But the line is too long and I cannot queue. And break time would be over before I could even get to the front."

"I could buy for you," Joachim said. "If you want."

"No, thanks. I don't want your money."

"Oh, no no," he said, then chuckled like an adult. "I have a . . . back door? Like, a person I can ask to go around the line and get us the snacks you want to buy. With your money."

"Oh?" Cece was suddenly paying attention. "Like, you know the seller?"

"Well . . ." He cocked his head, wondering if he should tell, then deciding in the affirmative. "My granny owns the canteen, actually."

Cece's eyebrows went up. "Really?"

"Really. So, I can, like, walk in. And then buy anything I want from inside. Here." He put out his hand. "Gimme your money, and tell me what you want, and I'll get it for you."

Cece obliged, much too preoccupied to give it further thought. Off Joachim went, leaving her alone to continue to ponder what would become of her one and only friendship.

Joachim was back in a jiffy. In his hand was her meat pie and can of soda, as well as an apple. She hadn't actually asked for the apple, which she told him.

"Oh no, I just got that one for you," he said. "You know. Back door, as I said. Also, balanced diet. You need fruits for that."

"Hmm." Cece set the food aside. "Thanks."

"Aren't you going to, like, eat?"

She looked him up and down. "Aren't you?"

He shrugged. "I eat early, and fast. Then I get the rest of break time to, well, play." He looked away, at the crowd of students milling around. "Not like these ones are interested in half the things I have to say anyway."

"Hmm."

"Are you . . . okay?" He perched next to her, but didn't really sit, like he wasn't sure. "Is something . . . the matter?"

"I don't even know," Cece said, and sighed. "I'm not even . . . sure."

"Do you want to . . . talk about it?"

"No." She picked up her meat pie, looked at it, then unwrapped it slowly. "If it's okay, I think I just want to be quiet and think today."

"Okay." He rose.

"You can—" She looked at him. "You can sit if you want."

"Oh." He sat. "Okay."

The two of them spent the rest of break time in silence.

CHAPTER FIVE

ONCE CECE GOT INTO THE car at the end of the school day, Iya asked the same question she always did, which, frankly, was starting to get a little bit old.

"Second week of secondary school, eh, dearest?" she said. "Feel like a big girl yet?"

"Iya!" Cece said. "Repeating the same thing over and over makes it, like, boring, you know, right?"

"Ha," her mother said and laughed and pulled out of the school parking lot. "Only two weeks, and look at you already with a smart mouth, calling me old and boring." She paused. "What's that look on your face, though? Did anything happen?" She angled her head. "Wait, you made any friends yet?"

Cece thought back to her interaction with Joachim. "I—don't know? Maybe? I met a boy—"

"Ooh, meeting boys already, are we?" Her mother raised an eyebrow. "Maybe you're taking this big-girl thing a little too seriously now, love."

"Eew, Iya," Cece said. "First, he only helped me buy lunch because the line was too long. And then . . . we didn't even talk or anything. We just . . . sat there."

"Well, that's a start. Sometimes the best friendships are forged in silence."

"Nah, I think it was just awkward."

Her mother chuckled, and then they stared at the road together for a bit.

"It takes awhile, dearest," Iya said, finally. "Friendships are not always easy. They have up-and-down moments, but that's okay. You'll still end up making good friends, old and new. And your old friendships never really go away. You simply discover a new place for them. Speaking of which . . ." Iya put her hand in her bag, rummaged around for something. "Therese did send you a message, or something—I can't—"

"When?" Cece's eyes widened. "How? Where is it?"

"It's on the family tablet." Iya was peering into her bag again, taking her eye off the road for a moment. "I thought I left it in the car after you used it this morning, but I think I must've taken it inside."

"What did she say? Did she—"

"I don't know, I didn't read it. Something about your game, or whatever." Iya gave up the search with a huff. "You'll see it when we get home."

The usually short drive home from Gemshore Secondary suddenly felt like a cross-country trip for Cece. She bounced on the seat of her buttocks, unable to stay put, wondering what the message from Therese was. *Is she angry? Does she not want to be friends anymore?* Anticipation bit at Cece like a gnat.

As soon as they pulled into their driveway, Cece flew out of the car and raced to the house, not hearing her mother call out for her to take off her uniform before she did anything else, or that she had left her backpack in the car. The tablet, on the dining table, beckoned like a shining, pulsing, magical square.

Her eyes devoured the text message notification—*notifications*, actually, as there were a series of them.

So sorry, Cece! the first text message read. *Dad says he cannot resubscribe to our Realms cos he's lost contact with the guy who was helping him do it, and now the new subscriptions are too expensive! We've lost Silver Oaks Park forever, OMG! :(*

Cece heaved a sigh of relief. *Reesa doesn't know.* She had been planning an apology all day long, but now she didn't need to use it.

But would that be, like, lying to Reesa? She put the thought away for the moment and flicked on to the next message.

So, another thing: my bro Hashim has made some new friends here, older boys like him. But one of them likes Minecraft and has introduced me to this group he plays with—they're so cool! They build their own servers and stuff.

Cece frowned, starting to remember the reasons why she had trashed Silver Oaks.

"Cecelia," Iya called in her Serious Voice as she came into the house. "Go get you stuff from the car, *now.*"

"I'm coming, coming," Cece said, moving on to the next message.

They wanted me to join them on this private server they run. And . . . don't be mad at me for this . . . but I joined them. I'm so sorry! Silver Oaks is already gone, and I really didn't just want to abandon everything we built together. But I'm just trying to make new friends . . .

"I'm not asking you again," Iya said. "And if I lock the car, don't come ask me for the keys."

Cece slammed the tablet on the table and went past her perplexed mother to get her stuff from the car. She slammed the door when she was done, and when she came back in, she dumped her backpack on the floor and sat on the couch, arms crossed, brow furrowed.

"What is *wrong* with you — this girl?" Iya muttered, and pressed the car lock on her keys, the car responding with a *beep-beep* outside. "You're not the first person to lose a friend, you know? And have you thought that maybe Therese is unhappy about losing a friend, too?"

Then she wouldn't be making new ones so soon, Cece thought, and eyed the tablet. The notification light continued to blink, meaning there were more messages to be read. Cece kissed her teeth, then plucked the tablet from the table and tapped the message. Her mother shook her head and left the room.

Anyway, don't worry! We can rebuild everything! I've begged them to allow you to join us in this new server they've put together — it's in a world they call Haven. Here, I've sent you the server address.

Cece didn't bother to look at the message with the invite. Instead, she navigated to the Minecraft application, opened its menu, and simply selected: Uninstall.

Cece did not look at the tablet for another two days. When she finally did, it was to play other games. She avoided her console entirely. There were other games loaded on her unit that she could play, too, but they were boring and single-player and she had played a lifetime of games alone. She did not need that anymore.

At school, she did not hang out with Joachim during break. She ate alone, and hid whenever she saw him hanging around, looking for someone to chat with. She did say hi to a few people, but none of those casual greetings ever crystallized into anything noteworthy, and she wasn't even interested in any kind of significant friendship right now, anyway. She was not looking to replace Therese, even if she didn't care for Therese anymore as she used to. What was the point of making new friends? They were only going to leave her after a while and become friends with some "cool" new people.

On the fourth day, though, something happened at the Alao household that caused Cece to reevaluate that approach.

"I think Mr. Njinga has changed to a new US number, finally," Baba said at the dinner table that day. "I cannot seem to reach him on his roaming Nigerian number anymore."

Cece's ears whipped to attention.

"Oh, really?" Iya said, and pulled out her phone, scrolling up and down, then dialed and listened for a moment. "Huh, that's true. It's telling me the same thing. *This number is no longer in service.*"

"What does that mean?" Cece asked. "Can I still message Therese through her father's number?"

"Oh, dearest," Iya said, and angled her head in a pitiful manner. "It would appear that is no longer possible."

All night, Cece tossed and turned in bed. She realized, now, how silly her tantrums had been. Iya had been right—her best friend had probably been struggling with the same thing she was. And Cece had pushed her away, destroyed the world they had built together, all because what—she had been frustrated? And whether Therese knew what Cece had done or not, she didn't seem to be upset. All she wanted was to continue to be Cece's friend.

But now that was impossible, because Therese was cut off phone-wise.

Unless . . .

Cece rose from bed, went to the living room, and retrieved the tablet before getting back into bed. The last message from Therese was still there.

Here's the URL. See you in Haven!

But there were even more messages after that.

Oh, wait, some info: you will spawn somewhere different, outside of Haven. But the admins have designed it so that every new joiner will have to complete three Tests. So you, too, will have to complete the three Tests to find Haven—well, to find Haven, and then me.

Tests? Cece frowned. *What is this girl talking about?* Cece scrolled down. There was one more message.

The Tests aren't entirely impossible or anything, especially if you have help to complete them like I did. But they can be tough, so just text me if you need help.

The last message was less instructional and more . . . sweet.

I trust you, Cece. You are the toughest person I know, so I know you will succeed. We will have Silver Oaks Park again, you and I. Best friends forever.

It almost brought tears to Cece's eyes. Therese still cared for her, still wanted to be her best friend, even though she had met new and cool Scottsdale people. Now Cece had a chance—a last chance, perhaps—to not lose her friend. And she was going to take it.

I'm sorry, Cece typed. *I spoiled everything because I was angry. But I will make it better. I will come to Haven.*

She pressed Send, but the message did not leave. Instead, it showed a red alert sign that read: This message could not be delivered to this number.

"Wonderful," Cece said to herself in the dark. There was no way she could contact her friend, then, even for help completing these so-called Tests. But no worries. Therese wanted her to come to Haven, and that was exactly what she was going to do.

It took awhile for the Minecraft application to re-download, and once it did, Cece opened it again and logged in. The old, expired Realm remained there. Cece deleted it from her list. That was the old Cece and the old world now. Today, she and Therese were going to start something new, and she was ready to make space for that.

She tapped the tab that said Servers, selected Add Server, and entered the server address that Therese had offered. She tapped Done afterward.

A new server appeared, titled: *Anarchia.*

What a name, Cece thought, then double-tapped it.

Connecting to external server . . . Join?

Cece tapped.

Encrypting . . .

Generating world . . . Locating server

Generating world . . . Loading resources

Generating world . . . Loading terrain

Welcome to Anarchia.

PART TWO

ANARCHIA AND THE OCURY

CHAPTER SIX

WHEN I SPAWN INTO THE world, the first thing I notice is how dark it is.

My last experience at Silver Oaks makes me want to not be in the dark for a while. Back when Therese was still around, we hung out some nights, upstairs on the balcony of our mansion. Mostly, we'd sit around and just chat, trying to name the kind of moon that was out in the sky. *This is a full moon. That's a quarter moon. No, that's gibbous. Wait, is it supposed to be a crescent moon? How come it's so square!*

This night, this darkness here, is the complete opposite of that. I am alone, to start. But the sky is also not the deep, dark blue of night. It's a deep red. The moon sinks into it, giving off a reddish ring, like a Frisbee soaked in juice. The moon also doesn't cast enough light to make it easy to see, hence the suffocating darkness.

"Okay," I say out loud to myself. "First thing, Cece: survive the night."

I could never achieve this back when I started playing Survival alone. Somehow, before I finished gathering the resources I needed to settle in for the night—mostly wood and coal—the day would end, night would come, and zombies and spiders and skeletons would spawn out of nowhere. I never survived a night any distance from my base.

Which was why I ended up deciding to play Peaceful and Peaceful alone. I'm not sure what difficulty this place is set to yet—it doesn't tell me—but it doesn't matter anyway. It's already night, and that means I'm already in danger. I have two choices: find some shelter quickly—preferably one that has already been built—or build one myself. Which means I will have to get the number one resource: wood.

I look in my inventory and, to no surprise, find it absolutely empty.

"Wood it is, then."

But I can barely see my own hands, not to mention what's around me. And for a lack of coal, I cannot build a torch to see, either. So, I have a third option: stand still, do not move, hope daylight comes fast, and no monsters spawn nearby or wander over. Then, when all the monsters are gone, I can go find myself some resources to begin this quest.

So, I do exactly just that. I stand there and wait for it to become daylight, trying to identify the moon like back then. This one looks strange—it seems like a full moon, but instead of a full square, it looks triangular. There are also no stars, which I find odd. It feels like I'm in another game altogether.

The ticks are adding up, and soon, the sky changes.

But instead of gradually changing to sunrise or dawn, the moon swiftly drops on the eastern horizon and then hangs there: half-gone, half-shining. And then the sun—if I can call it that—

comes up on the eastern horizon and hangs there as well, just like the moon. Both sit there on the horizon, side by side like friends who refuse to leave each other. It's like the sunrise is frozen in time—or is it the sunset?

Because of the red sky, sun and moon shine as one, sporting a vibrant reddish-orange. The light around has also increased, though it's still low, the little light of sunset. But it's enough for me to see what is around me for the first time.

Before me is a wasteland. Bare and open and lacking anything useful. Just darkness in every direction, rising and falling in different elevations of haphazard blocks. No trees for wood, no mountains for stone and coal, no materials for tools, weapons, or light. Just a lot of nothing.

"Jokers," I say, of the admins of this world.

I start to move, in whatever direction. After a while, I dig up a few blocks of what is beneath me and find it to be ordinary sand. From here, I can also see some out-of-place blocks: a random cobblestone block between two of sand, or a lonely gravel block that shouldn't be found at this elevation. I add it to my inventory, just so I can have something there. This is a land of always-darkness.

In this near darkness, I come upon my first object: a mob spawner.

It just sits there, solitary.

For a moment, I'm excited by the sight of it, a cage of burning fire. Then I recognize it from the reading I'd done a long time ago, when I was still trying to play Survival Mode on Easy or Normal. I remember now that I have only a few seconds before a new mob will spawn from it.

So I turn about and run.

I don't get very far. Just as I jump down two, three blocks, the sun swiftly dips again, and the moon turns reddish and triangular like before. Full darkness engulfs me. But this time, in this darkness, I'm not alone.

Eyes of various colors open before me.

The mob that gets me is not the first one I see — an Enderman. Its magenta eyes are a dead giveaway, even if I don't see the floating black limbs of the monster. But as I jump farther and farther away from the mob spawner, more eyes open up about me, these ones red, and multiple.

Spiders.

I don't even get a chance to count how many eyes there are — two? two thousand? — before they converge on me, skittering across the dirt. Their sucking sounds come together in a chorus as they attack, hisses of pain escaping my lips with each hit, until I am no more.

I respawn at the start point of emptiness.

The sun and moon are still occupying their double positions on the eastern horizon, half-shining, side by side. If I have to guess, they will be there only until the next darkness. I cannot calculate how long any of this lasts — more than a day? Less? But at least now I'm beginning to understand that this world does not operate by the usual rules. There will never be daylight, it seems. Only slightly dark and darkly dark. Sunset and night, each about half the length of a regular day.

It would be unwise for me to expect things to happen normally here.

With that in mind, I immediately go in the opposite direction of my last attempt.

Really puts the "waste" in "wasteland," I think. Because there's nothing much else in this opposite direction, either, other than more barrenness and a few lonely cactus plants. After a while of walking, I stop, confused. Is this a cruel joke that Therese and her friends are playing on me? Maybe it's time to leave and give up this quest to find Therese.

Then I remember: there's one last thing I can try. Something else I'd learned from my readings. *Stupid me!* Why didn't I think of this all along?

I call up my chatbox and enter:

[/locate]

As far as I remember, this will help me find the nearest of any possible generated structure. But the trick is that I'll have to try to guess what may be the most likely one.

Since where I am feels more like a desert, with all this dirt and whatnot, I try [temple] for any sort of pyramid. Nothing. So I try for tools or other resources using [buriedtreasure]. Nothing. I try for everything else I can remember: [mineshaft], [monument], even [shipwreck]. Nothing.

But then I try [village], and suddenly, it works. A bunch of co-ordinates jump out at me.

Not a wasteland after all, I think. Then I look at the location numbers and see how far away it is from my spawn point of 0, 0, 0—*very* far. Far enough that I'd be walking for days in the dark before I get there. Which also means, of course, that without light in this always-dark world, I'd be monster meat before I even make it a quarter of the way there.

Then I remember another trick from my readings: teleportation.

I enter the [/tp] command.

Ordinarily, this shouldn't work. It didn't work back then in Silver Oaks, when Therese and I tried it. Technically it's a cheat, and cheats were disabled in Silver Oaks.

But this is a much weirder world, built by people who know what they're doing, as Therese said. They're likely to have cheats turned on or a mod installed that allows them to do weird things.

So I take a gamble: I add the numbers for the location and send.

The world about me flips, and suddenly I am no longer standing in a wasteland, but in a serene and peaceful village, filled with trees and houses and water and everything I'd ever need to survive in this dark, dark world.

It worked! I scream internally.

The village is an empty and quiet little collection of buildings, tucked away from the wastelands around my spawn point. Maybe a little bit too quiet, it dawns on me now, as I look around and see no sign of life, just like in the wastelands. In fact, the buildings look deserted, like ruins but not ancient. Some buildings look half-built, abandoned halfway. The basic wheat and potato farms have been cleaned out, likely by marauders passing through, or maybe just lost souls like me looking for something to eat.

But the most important question here is this: Where did everyone *go*?

As soon as I think this, a flash of movement zips past the corner of my vision. I turn about, expecting to see a monster of some sort, something fast maybe like new spiders, or a creeper creeping up on me, ready to explode. Maybe even a villager, wandering off.

Instead, what I see is a . . . person?

Another player, actually. I know this because a villager would never wear armor. And especially not diamond armor. She also has a diamond sword, which she holds at the ready. There's no name tag over her head—it seems one of this server's mods has turned them off by default. Mine also just says **anonymous**, though it gives me the option to reveal my actual name tag, **cece_lao**, in chat if I want.

A *person, though!* My mind cannot contain the joy that I instantly feel. *Finally!* Someone to take me around, tell me what's what, help explain how I can best find resources and everything else I'll need to find my way to Haven and Therese.

I open up my chatbox and select the whisper command for messaging nearby players.

"Hi!" My voice-to-text mod writes the message in for me. Therese and I got it early on from her dad, who got it from his server hosting guy, who said he'd made it for player ease. Before the message sends off, I make sure to reveal my name tag in chat. Hopefully, that will be a signal of friendship to this stranger in a strange land.

The girl doesn't respond. Just stands there, unmoving.

"I'm Cece," I continue, "but you already know that from my name tag, haha. OMG, it's so great to see another person in this forsaken place! Are you one of Therese's new friends?"

The player puts away her sword in exchange for a bow and arrow, which appears swiftly in her hand. She holds it, but not at the ready, more like inquisitively. I try again.

"I have so many questions. My friend—her name's Therese—she invited me to this world, to find a place called Haven . . ."

"Haven," the girl says finally, barely showing any change in her composure. The text-to-voice narrator function reads her words back to me. She, too, chooses to reveal her name tag in chat. **WereDragon_86**, it says.

"Yes, Haven! And she said something about a few Tests—"

"Tests," the girl says.

"Yes, exactly! Said if I complete them I could find my way to Haven. Any idea where I can find them?"

"Find the Tests," the girl says.

"Yes," I say. "Are they in this village, or another place? I didn't see any other location when I—"

The girl raises her bow and arrow and points it at me. I don't even have time to be surprised before the first arrow strikes. But I guess what does surprise me is that she doesn't stop, doesn't even give me time to run away. She fires the next arrow, and the next, and the next, all with practiced ease. Even by the third arrow, when I've managed to catch on to the fact that she means to kill me, running away is moot.

I take maybe five, six steps before the last arrow hits me and the world folds again.

CHAPTER SEVEN

I SPAWN BACK IN THE wastelands. For a moment, I'm too shocked to do anything but stand there in the dark.

Did I just get killed by a . . . player? And the more important question: Why?

Of course, I've always known there are players out there who take joy in fighting other players rather than building things and battling with hostile mobs, but I never thought I would see one. Especially not out here in this server—not with the way Therese had described Haven, and the quest for it.

But I can't stay out here in the wastelands, either, because I'll get eaten soon enough. So I do what I already know will work: I teleport back into the village.

WereDragon is still there, almost as if she has simply been waiting for my return. Just like the last time, she doesn't lift the arrow just yet, and simply stands there, observing me, as if surprised or confused by my arrival, or both.

"Wait," I say. "I come in peace."

"Haha" is her only response.

"No, really," I say. "I have no weapons, no food, no tools, no resources. I've literally just dropped in, and I was only able to come here because teleport is enabled."

"And you chose to come *here?*" There's a sense of incredulity I don't see expressed on the flat face of her avatar. "To the hunting grounds?"

"*Hunting?*" I say. "The location said this was, like, just an ordinary village."

There's a pause before she says: "You really are a noob, aren't you?"

I would shrug if I could. "Kinda. But I'm just here to meet my friend. As I said, she's in Haven. If you can point me in the direction of it, that'll be awesome."

I bet she would cackle if she could, too, from the way she says, "Point you in the direction of Haven, is it?"

"Yes. Just that. And maybe tell me anything I need to know to not get, you know, killed or something."

"Hmm," she says. Another pause. "Okay, then."

"Okay?"

"Yes, okay. But on one condition."

"What's that?"

"I get to kill you right after."

Now it's my turn to pause. "Excuse me?"

"Yeah," says WereDragon, tucking in her bow. "I tell you everything you need to know about Anarchia, and about Haven, and then I kill you right after."

It sounds like an odd trade, one that doesn't seem even to me. What does she get out of killing me? Is there something I should be paying attention to here that I'm not?

But I won't be able to learn that, or anything else about this place, if I don't agree to it either way.

"All right," I say. "Fine."

"Come on, then," she says, moving away and leading me somewhere. "Follow my exact footsteps, slowly. I may get to kill you, but at least I'll be more gentle than the mobs, if you wake them up."

WereDragon takes me past the corridors between some buildings and some trees, stopping every now and then to wait and listen. At first, I don't know what we're looking for, so I'm looking around, too, but she tells me to not turn my head unless she tells me to. Only after we have done this three times do I realize that at each of these points, we have gone past a haunting of Endermen, and she has just saved me from looking directly into their purple eyes and provoking them to attack us.

After some more darting and dodging, we get to a small lake. We pause here again for some of the zombies hanging around to turn their backs to us, then we slip past them and go into the water. Once under, a block or two down, past the sand and into the sandstone, WereDragon pulls out a pickaxe and starts to hack at the sandstone. Her excavation is super slow now that we're fully submerged in water, but she seems experienced and does it quickly enough. Multiple sandstone blocks soon give way and we enter into the space made by them.

A room—a sort of dungeon—lit by torches.

Water flows in, but that's no bother. WereDragon stacks the broken blocks back and blocks off the water flow, and soon enough, the water that has flown in is gone.

"So," she says, opening a chest and dropping a bunch of things inside. "You want to know about Anarchia."

"Yes," I say, looking around. "What *is* this place?"

"If you mean this room," she says, "it's an underground bunker I built a long time ago, so I can run and hide if I get cornered by players or mobs here."

"Why not just go into a house in the village and hide?"

I sense her scoff at the question, even if she doesn't actually scoff.

"Because a player will simply just teleport outside your door and kill you while you're AFK," she says. "A house in the village is the worst place to be, because it's a trap. There's nowhere to run to if an Anarchian corners you in there."

She finishes putting stuff into the chest and turns to face me. "Now, if you meant to ask about Anarchia—what this place '*is*'— you might want to sit down for that."

There's no sitting down, of course, so we stand next to each other, and she tells me everything.

Anarchia, this abandoned world you see, was once a fun and thriving place. In fact, all of it was once named Haven, not just a tiny slice. It was an open server, a free world where everyone popped in and had fun. There used to be cool creations like tree houses and a mock space shuttle. Everyone came here to make new friends. And though there were both hostile and neutral mobs to be fought, we fought them together.

Then a shadowy admin called the Ocury got their hands on the server, and everything changed.

The rules were the first to go. The Ocury installed various mods, and soon, day turned to everlasting night. One day, there was the sun; the next day, we had only sunset and night. And with everlasting night came the mobs, more of them than we had ever seen in this world. Worse, the Ocury put mob spawners everywhere they could, so that it's become impossible to spawn anywhere and not run into a mob or two, no matter the direction one goes in.

Many other rules were changed. It's impossible to find your way anywhere, for instance, unless you make your own map. Some players do that by drawing on paper, if you can find it—paper is super scarce here. The Ocury added a mod that lets you draw or write directly on it. But you need to know the whole place to draw a correct map, right? Exactly. So most of us just keep running into trouble and getting attacked by mobs or other players all the time. The only place without mobs—a small slice of paradise left in a corner of this world—is a place the Ocury has now named Haven. But the Ocury has also made it inaccessible to every player, except those who pass the Haven Trials.

Those three "Tests" you spoke of earlier? Those are the Haven Trials. Every quester gets five lives to traverse Anarchia and make it into the serene safety of Haven. I've lost three lives so far, and have only two left. Five tries is all we get. If you don't make it to Haven by the fifth attempt, then you will be banned from this server forever.

The Trials themselves are not simple, either. So far, I've not heard of anyone who has been able to complete them alone, without help from other players. Your friend must have had help to cross over into Haven, yes? Well, we can't ask her now, because once you get into Haven, the Ocury blocks you from contacting any other players here so that they can't tell you the tricks or anything.

Now, you asked why I need to kill you, yes? Well, this is it: I'm an Anarchian. You know what that means? It means we are citizens of this world, and we understand its rules and live by them. Don't go out at night. Learn to build quick shelters so you can quickly hide once sunset ends. But most important, if you see another player, run.

The Ocury has made it so that every time you defeat another player, you get XP—experience points. A good chunk of them, in fact. You maybe don't care about collecting yours. But I care. I've been carefully gathering XP for a while. You know why?

Because the ultimate prize for unlocking a huge amount of XP is to become the next Ocury. And if I can do that, then I can take control of the server and replace the current one.

That's right. The Ocury is replaceable. But only if you can defeat enough fellow players and rack up the right XP. Something tells me the Ocury does this to prevent players from making it to Haven—if they have to fight one another, no one gets there!

I don't care. I want to be the next Ocury anyway. Someone has to do it. We all deserve a place like Haven without having to battle for it, right? That's what I'm going to do, once I can gather enough XP to become the Ocury myself. I'm going to make everywhere like Haven.

I hear that once you complete the Third Trial, you get a bunch of XP. But there's a catch: once you make it into Haven, you can't come back to Anarchia. Not unless you're the Ocury yourself or something. So if I don't amass enough XP while I'm here—I hear you need at least fifteen thousand or something—then I can never get any more, because there's no XP in Haven, just . . . joy, I guess. If I'm going to make all of Anarchia like Haven, I need to get as much XP here as I can, and take it to Haven with me. Or at least to that Third Trial, where I hear you can get thousands just for completing it.

Anyway, here's what you need to know: if the mobs don't get you, the Trials will. If the Trials don't get you, Anarchians will. Either way, you die five times, you're out. Forever.

If this seems harsh, that's because the Ocury made it so. Anarchia is a bitter land with a hard outlook. Except if you make it to Haven, of course, and then you're all roses and mint. But until then, you will have to fight hard here—either to protect yourself, or to make friends who will.

I had friends, once, but they chose to betray me, all for some XP. Now, I have chosen to protect myself. Which is why, I'm sorry to say this—I have to kill you.

Okay, that's it. Here, eat this—your hunger bar looks down . . . Satisfied? Good. Now turn around while I draw my sword.

CHAPTER EIGHT

BACK AT GEMSHORE SECONDARY THE morning after her traipse through the wastelands of Anarchia, Cece could barely concentrate in class. A part of that was because though most of the subjects—like math, English, and social studies—were familiar, many of them were completely new. There was agricultural science, whose teacher talked a lot about farms. Business studies was another new one that seemed like it should be important but she couldn't figure out why. And then there were the local languages, specifically Yoruba, whose teacher stood in front of her this morning, yapping on and on. Cece couldn't quite speak the language yet, but could partially understand what the woman was saying because her parents spoke Yoruba between themselves in the house, sometimes even to her.

But she tuned the woman out anyway, because her mind was really somewhere else, far away in the world of Anarchia.

After WereDragon_86 had told her everything she needed to know—and then promptly killed her off—she had gone to bed, her mind filled with questions.

How do I get to Therese now without getting killed? She had only two lives left out of her initial five, and had zero weapons, food, resources, or whatever. There was no way to contact Therese and ask her how she had done it. As WereDragon had said, there were only two options: make friends, or gather the right resources. The second was going to be hard without knowing what to do, and after losing more than half her lives, she wasn't ready to simply go out there and risk it.

Making friends was the other option, but, well, how did that work out for her last time? She had died—twice!—while trying to do so. So that was a no-go as well.

But there was a third option, at least, it seemed. She could hide.

She had watched the way WereDragon moved, slipping away in the dark and hiding, making sure to stay out of sight of everything and everyone. She could do that, too, couldn't she? She could make her way to Haven that way.

"Miss Alao," someone was saying, jerking Cece back to the present. Cece realized she'd been looking through the window, her gaze fixated outside.

"Something of interest out there that you want to share with the class?" the Yoruba teacher, a dark-skinned and slightly chubby woman, said. Then she repeated the question in Yoruba.

"No, ma," Cece said, suddenly feeling very small and noticed. Especially when people in the class chuckled and giggled.

"No?" the teacher said. "Then maybe you should go out and look for it," she said, waving her duster at Cece. "Go on. Stand outside in the sun and remain there, where I can see you."

So Cece went out and stood in the sun, where she simply continued to think about how she was going to have to find a way to deal with all these Haven Trials, whatever they ended up being.

She thought about how she would find her way around without a map of some sort, or what it would take to get someone to give her that information.

Soon, the bell rang for break time, and Cece realized the Yoruba teacher had forgotten to release her from her punishment. She stood there, unsure if she was allowed to leave, as her fellow students spilled out of classrooms and into the playground.

"Still standing there, child?" someone said, and she looked and saw it was the girl from the first day, the one whom Joachim had called Ofure. Cece ignored her, caught in two minds about whether to stay or go.

"You know you can leave, right?" another voice said, and this one was Joachim, coming up to her. "Everyone knows that all punishments are erased once it's break time. Come, I'll get us something to eat."

Cece nodded, then followed, but within her, more conflict brewed. Everyone somehow knew everything—where to go, what to do, how to do it. Everyone, it seemed, except her.

For my fourth attempt at starting the Haven Trials, I decide to sneak my way through Anarchia. More hiding, less stumbling into people or mobs. Less dying.

Once I land at the spawn point, I teleport straight to the village and follow the exact same patterns that WereDragon did. I'm just trying to avoid bumping into any new players, as well as to evade all the mobs I spot in the growing dark—spiders, Endermen, zombies, skeletons, at least one creeper. So, of course, I get lost soon enough.

Wonderful, I think, looking around. *How do I get out of here if I don't even know where I'm going?*

So I do the one thing WereDragon told me not to do: I go into the nearest house.

It's like most village houses, which means it's empty, so I take the free space to think about my next step. The next logical thing would be to get resources. I might be trying to sneak around to Haven, but I'll still need tools, food, even weapons, to make my way through.

First thing will be to find a good place to reset my spawn point, instead of spawning into the wastelands each time and having to teleport all the way here. There's no sleeping in this server, clearly, so a spawn point reset command should be fine. It won't be in this house, though, as WereDragon has already warned me of the dangers of waking up to Anarchians lying in wait.

I peek outside, and once the coast is clear, I dash for the nearest tree line I can find. I hide there, watching out for any movement. Nothing registers, so I start to mine.

The trees are birch, and after a bit of mining, I get a good chunk of wood to make a crafting table. I dash back into the house and quickly make the table, then a wooden pickaxe.

Next resource: light.

I already know that placing torches down will attract players, but I need light to find my way regardless. Besides, I hear that hostile mobs have a chance of spawning in the dark with every tick of time, so if I'm going to move a lot in the night, I'll need light to prevent that from happening close to me.

A conundrum, isn't it?

The torch I find is only two houses down, and I soon realize that I'm lucky to get one so close, because most of the torches here seem to have been removed. I have to circle around a group of skeletons to get there, but I do so anyway, and soon enough, I have two torches in my inventory.

Next step: food.

Perhaps this is what WereDragon meant by this place being a hunting ground. After moving about a bit, dodging between houses and behind some more trees, I discover there are zero passive mobs around. Perhaps the *"hunting"* part was really about getting meat from the chickens, sheep, cows, and pigs, and not just about hunting players and mobs.

While I'm still searching, I stumble upon a very disturbing sight.

In the low light of sunset, I see a player—a boy. Not very well-armored, and with no weapons in hand, either. He's dressed in a wacky way, though, with spiky hair and wearing a red mask that covers his eyes, like a superhero. The rest of his chosen skin is wacky too, a brown-and-gray design that looks like something out of a garage. But what's more important is what he's doing: striking an animal. *Ooh, some meat,* I think, before I realize that is not the case.

The animal he's striking is a cat. And surprisingly, the cat's not taking damage or dying, but just standing there and withstanding the blows.

That doesn't stop the boy, though. He just keeps striking and striking and striking. Each time the cat racks up a certain amount of blows, it *rawrs* and makes a face, but it doesn't strike back. It looks unshapely, the cat, like there's something wrong with it, like it's not built right. It's an orange animal, but not a tabby, and looks striped like a small tiger.

The boy keeps striking the cat.

"Hey!" I call out, forgetting where I am, forgetting my plans to sneak through and stay as quiet as possible. "Hey, you, stop that!"

The boy raises his head and looks toward the trees I'm hiding behind, trying to find me in the low light, but not really seeing me. I wonder if he'll come over to check, or pull up his own loca-tor and—

Out of nowhere, an arrow flies and strikes the boy in the chest. And then a horde of skeletons spawn and descend upon him.

I stay hidden, watching it all.

It doesn't take long for him to fail at fighting them off. Some-how, his striking the cat seems to have attracted the skeletons, and out of nowhere, a good chunk of them appear. The boy pulls out a bow and arrow and fires one, two, three shots, gets a skeleton or two. By the time he's finished with all seven skeletons, they are finished with him, too. He falls, disappears, and his whole inven-tory drops to the ground.

The cat has not moved.

I wait a minute or two before emerging from my hiding place. The resources are still scattered all around—so many of them! Everything I'm looking for: meat, wheat, coal, iron, seeds, even fish and apples. I pick them all up, including the boy's bow and arrow. The skeletons he's killed have dropped bones, and I pick those up, too. One skeleton has dropped an extra arrow, which I add to my inventory.

There is one last piece of inventory the boy has dropped. When I pick it up, I can't believe what I'm looking at.

It's a map.

Whoa, I think. *Tough luck, dude.*

With the map now in my inventory, I turn my attention to the cat. It has still not moved, just standing there. I remember reading somewhere that cats eat salmon or cod? Well, this cat is in luck, because I happen to have two pieces of salmon in my newly stocked inventory. I pull them out and hand them over.

The cat is slow in accepting, grouchy, purring in a way that's crabby but not menacing. After a long while, it takes the first salmon and gobbles it up. Then it does the same with the next.

A flurry of hearts appears above its head.

When I turn to go, it follows me. All the way to the nearest house, making a lot of noise that thankfully doesn't attract any hostiles. *My sneaking days are over*, I think, which pleases me. I have a map now. I can teleport anywhere once I can figure out what's where.

I decide to take shelter in the house in order to make sense of the map and decode its information. Once inside, I pull it out, but find concentrating difficult, as the cat keeps getting in my way, following me with a *rawr* and making a face each time I try to shoo it away.

"Cranky," I say. "That's what I'll call you. Because you're just quarrelsome."

It responds with another *rawr*. I turn back to my map and wonder: What next?

CHAPTER NINE

DURING BREAK TIME AT SCHOOL the day after, Cece was back in her solo corner of the food court. She sat alone, buried elbow-deep in a printout of the terrain map she had picked up from the Anarchian.

It was, as she suspected, a playermade map of the whole of Anarchia, featuring the exact locations for the three Haven Trials. The Anarchian boy who had been smacking Cranky the cat had marked some points on the map, and it had taken Cece some time to figure out what each mark was.

She'd taken a screenshot of it with her tablet, then printed the screenshot out on paper so she could look at it at school. She had also spent last night marking some other locations that were important to her. In addition to the spots where the three Haven Trials had been marked, she'd marked different biomes.

She'd paid for all the time she'd spent getting this done by dozing through social studies class this morning. Luckily for her, the teacher had been too aloof to notice.

As she studied it some more in the food court now, Cece could see that her instinctive grouping of the map into three distinct areas—Desertland, Greenland, and Mountainland—had been right. However, the biomes each contained did not seem like those she would have expected them to. Greenland, for instance, contained both grassland and dark forest biomes. The grassland, where the village was located, looked like it was drying up. Desertland, large and sprawling next to Greenland, seemed to be encroaching upon the grasslands' greenery.

The Anarchian boy had marked only a few spots in Greenland: the village and two other spots. The first of these, a small body of water, Cece realized was the place where WereDragon's underwater hideout was. The second was a place he'd marked **Dark Forest**. The third spot, marked side by side with the forest, brought fear to Cece's heart. It read: **Woodland Mansion**. And beside it was written: **First Trial: Evoker**.

Cece had read about evokers, who were one kind of various non-player hostiles in Minecraft called illagers. Illagers attacked players and pretty much every human passive mob in sight. But evokers were special, in that they were spellcasters who could summon their own hostile mobs, a collection of armed, winged fighters called vexes. The vexes, once commanded, were sly and difficult to defeat. They could pass through any block, from water to lava to stone, without taking damage, and then sneak up on players. Cece had watched a few online videos of players fighting evokers, and just from the kind of weaponry, skill, and dexterity players had employed, she knew that trying to defeat an evoker was not going to be a walk in the park.

Desertland contained the desert wasteland in which she had first spawned in the game. Though bare-looking on the map, it had many more marks, almost triple the amount of those in Greenland. Many of these were marked as mob spawners, with only one marked differently. It read: **Second Trial.** It did not offer any explanation about what that might be.

Mountainland was not really an area of its own. Rather, it was a mountain range that separated the other two areas from a third empty gray space that did not seem to be a part of the map. There were no marks, notes, or land formations. The only thing written in that space were two large words: **NO TELEPORTING.** Next to that: **Third Trial?** The question mark was especially large.

Based on that alone, Cece deduced a few things. The location of the third and final Trial definitely had to be somewhere in Mountainland, or past it. She guessed it was impossible to get there without completing the first two Trials, since teleporting was enabled between Desertland and Greenland, but not into Mountainland. Perhaps it would be unlocked once she completed the first two Trials. If not, she would probably have to journey into Mountainland on foot. Either way, the journey would be unwieldy, and treacherous.

A loud bell rang somewhere, jolting Cece out of her reverie and signaling the end of break time. Cece packed up her map and hurried back toward class, her brain spinning like the inside of a clock. She somehow had to complete the three Haven Trials with nothing but her remaining two lives, a few basic resources, and a useless cat that insisted on following her around.

There was a lot of planning to do, and so little time to do the learning required for it. Getting to Therese, it seemed, was going to be the most uphill task she had ever embarked on in her life.

"Watchu looking at?"

It was the end of the school day and Cece was in the waiting area of the parking lot, waiting for Iya to come pick her up. She had pulled out her map again and was studying it, trying to think of ways to survive in this treacherous world on only two lives. Over her shoulder had come Joachim, poking his head into the paper.

"Oooh, what world is this?" he asked. "Never seen nothing like it."

"It's nothing," Cece said, and made to tuck it away.

"Doesn't make any sense, too," Joachim said, cleaning a spot on the bench she was sitting on and sitting next to her. "How come there's mob spawners in what looks like a desert?"

"Exactly!" Cece found herself saying. "And that's not the only thing—everything is messed up there, and nothing at all works."

"What did you call it again?"

"I didn't," Cece said, "but it's called Anarchia."

"Anarchia," he said. "Sounds super dangerous."

"Because it is."

"Then why go there? Why not just play something more fun and exciting? I like to play games on the easiest possible modes. I'm just all about having fun, not trying to have a heart attack."

"OMG, me, too!" Cece said. "But I have to find my friend, so I have to do it, and I have no idea how to complete this world."

"Well, if you ever need any help," said Joachim, "I'm always happy to brainstorm ideas with you."

So, Cece told him everything: about Therese leaving; about losing contact with her; about traversing Anarchia and meeting WereDragon and Cranky; and about the three Trials she had to complete to get to Haven and reunite with Therese.

Joachim listened intently and whistled loudly afterward.

"Wow," he said. "And you need to do all of this on two lives and a bow and arrow?"

"Impossible, right?" Cece said. "I know."

"Well, not really," said Joachim. "Did you say teleporting is enabled between Greenland and Desertland?"

"Yes."

"Then don't walk anywhere at all. Even if you don't know where you're going, teleport somewhere nearby instead and explore. Once you know you're safe, walk the rest of the way. The only places you should teleport to are your base and the Trials."

"I don't have a base," Cece said. "I can't even have one—there are hostile mobs and players everywhere."

"Then just make sure to set a spawn point in at least one safe and lit location," he said. "So you don't spawn in the middle of the desert every time, or get surprised again by players or mobs in the village."

"I know what a spawn point is for, Mr. I-Too-Know," said Cece.

Joachim held up his hands. "Sorry, sorry. I overexplain a lot, I know." He put out a hand. "Lemme see that map again."

Cece offered it to him, and he took a quick look.

"Aah, see right here," he said, pointing to the dark forest. "No player would want to go there, because it's always dark enough to spawn mobs, even with light outside, right? And it's near the First Trial, too! So, on your first teleport there, quickly build an underground shelter if you can—there'll be a lot of wood around for blockading it. You don't even need windows or doors, because it's always night anyway. Just build it somewhere underground, light it with a lot of torches, set your spawn point there, and voila, you have a base. Now you can always teleport from there to the village or to the Trials and back." He rubbed his hands together in satisfaction.

"What about the cat?"

"What cat?"

"Cranky. I told you, it follows me everywhere."

"Well, I guess if you teleport, you'll leave it behind. That's better, even. I'm not sure if you'd want to be dragging anything or anyone along on such a quest."

This sounded like the opposite of what Therese had said— that she'd need all the help she could get to cross to Haven. But she *was* getting help, wasn't she? First from WereDragon, though she had paid dearly for that. And now from Joachim, who had given her at least one solution to her problems. If she could indeed get a base near the First Trial, she could take some time to study her environment well enough to make it to the evoker and back without incident. If she *could* defeat the evoker and its vexes, of course.

"Thanks, Joachim," Cece said, smiling. "This will really help my quest."

"It's nothing," he said. "Also, you can call me Jo. Everyone does."

"Okay," Cece said, and sighed. "This game used to be fun. When it was just Therese and me in Silver Oaks. Now, it just feels like so much work. And so . . ."

"Alone?" Joachim said, looking wistful himself. "Yeah, for me, too, though I was not as big on building stuff as you two were. My friends from primary school and I, we liked to fight hostile mobs. Oooh, we'd find the nastiest ones and fight them, just because. We'd go find villages without iron golems and protect them from illagers." He sighed. "They've all moved away now or stopped playing for some other reason. Playing Minecraft alone is not as fun for me, and I don't want to play with random strangers on the internet. I haven't played Minecraft in a long time because of that."

Cece wanted to ask if he would like to play with her, then remembered she didn't have Silver Oaks anymore, and she didn't want to start a new world where it would be just the two of them. And she couldn't invite him to Anarchia, could she? It wasn't her server, to start with, and Therese had invited *her alone* to Haven. Also, wasn't he the one who said carrying someone along on such a quest would be difficult? It was just as well. She didn't even know him that well yet anyway.

Iya's car pulled into the lot just then, saving Cece from her dilemma. She rose, Iya's neck already craning in search of her.

"My mother is here," she said. "See you around."

"See you," Joachim said, and waved goodbye.

In the car, Iya was wearing a sly smile.

"Is that your new friend?" she asked.

"Yes," said Cece. "That's Joachim, but we call him Jo."

"Ooh, a nice name," Iya said, maneuvering to get a good look. "And a nice boy, too. Neat, and quiet from the look of things."

"Can we just go?" Cece said, but Iya was already pushing at the car horn, waving to Joachim. The boy looked up, surprised, but grinned and waved back. Cece groaned and slid down in her seat until she was below the window line.

"Just drive, Iya!" she said.

"Ooh, I'm embarrassing you, is it?" Iya said, pulling away. "I'm just glad that you made a nice friend, that's all. Maybe you can invite him to lunch, and we can get to know him even better."

Cece rolled her eyes. The last person she had invited to lunch was Therese, and look how that had ended up. There would be no more lunches until she found her way back to Therese. It would be a long, long time before she was ready to open up that space to someone else.

CHAPTER TEN

NOW ARMED WITH MUCH MORE information about Anarchia, I set out to complete the First Trial.

The game loads and I'm in the same house. Cranky is still there next to me, waiting on my next move. I make a mental note that I have still not set my spawn point yet, so if anything happens to me now, I'll respawn in Desertland, at the server's own spawn point.

I look through the window to see if there are any monsters or Anarchians outside. None nearby, from the look of things, but I do see some shining eyes in the distance. I duck back down and pet Cranky.

"Time to go now, friend," I say. "Not sure I can take you along on this one."

Cranky *rawrs* like cats usually do, and seems unbothered by the thought of being left behind. With that reassurance, I take out the map and look for the location of the dark forest.

My plan is this: with the First Trial located inside the dark forest itself, I will have to spawn just outside the forest and build my planned underground base there. Then I will teleport between the trial and my base as need be, coming back here to the village only when necessary.

The map tells me I will have to travel northwest from where I currently am to get to the forest. The dark forest is many, many blocks away, which means teleporting will be the quickest way to get there. The bad news, though, is that teleporting directly into a dark forest—even so close to the edge of it—is not a good plan. Hostile mobs are sure to be lurking behind every tree.

I take the location of the forest and subtract a good chunk of blocks south and east of it, so that I'll land in a location outside. Then I place this new location into the chatbox and send.

The world about me flips again, and I am dropped in a sea of gray nothingness.

Oh no, I think. *I have made wrong calculations and ended up somewhere else.*

But those fears are soon gone as everything about me starts to reveal, the world taking its time to come into view.

Before me is a rising level of grassland, green and spare in all directions, just like it was back at the village. The one difference, though, is that in the near distance I can see the dark forest, sprawling in every direction. And when I look up, in the center of the forest is a tall, exquisite-looking woodland mansion.

All the way from here, the mansion looks very much like the one Therese and I had back at Silver Oaks, if not even better. It's wide and tall, with deep-brown roofs, gray cobblestone walls, and many windows. I can tell, just by looking, that there'll be as many rooms as Therese and my mansion had, and that it'll probably take a long time to search the whole place.

I also realize that this is where the First Trial—and the evoker—are located.

Time to build my base and prepare, then, I think. Thankfully, this is the part that I'm good at—building.

It's almost night, which means the monsters will be out in full force soon if I don't get my act together. I go as close to the edge of the forest as I can to find a good spot for the base. I did enough of the work on Silver Oaks that I can remember everything I did while building our basement. I also remember that the best place to hide an underground house is next to an inconspicuous tree. Especially one that's situated among many at the edge of the forest.

I choose a spot beside a rise in the terrain that is covered by a lot of grass, and begin digging.

First, I need to build a staircase about nine blocks down, so that I can cover the whole house on top without it being easily found by a random person digging up just one block. But I don't have great resources like pistons to open up many blocks at once (we had a ton of these back at Silver Oaks). So instead, I'll have to make it easy to dig my way into the house and out anytime.

After digging the right amount of blocks, I place a torch on the staircase. Then I go back out and collect some wood from the edge of the forest. Making my staircase out of wood will make it easier for me to know where my staircase is if I ever become un-sure of the house's location. I could just randomly start digging and would know I'd reached my house once I reached wood.

The forest is scary, even just looking at it from here. It's not night out here yet, and all I can see is darkness in there. Far away, just within my view, are eyes, shining in the dark. I quickly look away, hoping they are not Endermen who have now locked eyes with me and who I will now be forced to battle.

Thankfully, none of this happens, and I gather enough wood to go back and drop a crafting table. Then I dig some more space, rebuild my stairs, and make a few more torches, one of which I place closer to the entrance of the stairs.

Then I close it all up from the top.

Okay, I think, standing there on the stairs. *Step one done. Now the hard part.*

It's not really the hard part, to be fair. Right now, all I need is one room.

I return to the bottom of the stairs and dig seven blocks—right, left, then inward. I leave torches at the end of each tunnel. Then afterward, I spend time on the backbreaking task of removing all the earth in between.

It takes awhile, but soon, I have a large, well-lit room underground, with stairs to the surface.

Basic, I think, *but it'll do.*

I place the crafting table in one corner. Then I craft four wooden chests, connecting two each together to make two double chests, and place those in another corner. To avoid losing my inventory in the event that I die, I place all my resources in the chests for now, to be retrieved as needed. As I place them, I count:

- 1 bow
- 16 arrows
- 11 chunks of coal
- 4 chunks of beef (raw)
- 4 chunks of beef (cooked)
- 1 chunk of pork (cooked)
- 3 chunks of mutton (raw)
- 12 apples

- 5 strips of wheat
- 3 blocks of raw iron
- 3 wheat seeds
- 9 sweet berries
- 24 blocks of wood
- 64 blocks of sand
- 64 blocks of dirt

The dirt and sand I leave in my inventory, and the rest I place in the chests. On second thought, and with one eye on my hunger bar after all that work I've done, I eat a chunk of cooked beef, an apple, and two sweet berries, which brings my resources on those items to:

- 3 chunks of beef (cooked)
- 11 apples
- 7 sweet berries

With that, I can now finally reset my spawn point, and plan my attack on the evoker in the woodland mansion.

CHAPTER ELEVEN

I WAKE UP READY FOR battle.

I start my preparation by ensuring I have the right resources and information for this fight. Based on my intel from the many hours of online videos I watched about evokers, I've learned that the trick to defeating them is to avoid close fights and to actually stay far away and shoot them with arrows. This is because evokers attack not just by summoning vexes, but by raising fangs from the floor that snap shut and try to eat you. Plus, they move very fast! Attacking the evoker from a distance means I can't get caught unawares by any of these attacks. Thankfully, I have just the weapon for that: my trusty bow. But I need another handheld weapon, just in case. So the first thing I do is craft a brand-new sword.

As I craft, I go over the plan in my head. Most players in the videos I watched were very happy to face the evoker head-on, because they had sophisticated weapons made from diamonds. Even with ranged fighting, all of them had the good stuff, like modified bows and enchanted arrows and whatnot. I, on the other hand, just have stone stuff, arrows included. So it was great to see one video in particular that offered an easier way to attack the evoker for someone like me with few resources.

The trick? Never enter the mansion.

Even without that video, I already knew this part. Every woodland mansion seems to have three floors or levels, which means I have to battle mobs all the way to the top, where the evoker is. But the video's trick involves sneak-attacking the evoker, who is likely to be in the room on the top floor, by climbing onto the roof from *outside*. Once there, I peep through a window and locate the evoker. If I'm lucky enough, they won't see me, and I break the glass and shoot them through the window. Four fully charged arrows on target is all I need to complete the first Haven Trial.

Sounds easy enough, except for one tiny problem: I'm bad at aiming.

In fact, I'm bad at fighting, period. In the heat of battle, I'm pretty sure it'll take me *a lot* of tries to get those four arrows to hit their target. Thankfully, I have sixteen arrows, which means four tries per hit for this hostile mob. My chances look good.

I don't know what I will do, though, if the evoker is able to close the distance in that time. I don't know what I will do if they have enough time to release vexes, which can pass through the walls and get to me. I don't know if this is a fight I'll win. But I have to try.

I climb the stairs, cut through two blocks of grass, and poke my head out. It is sunset, which means fewer or no mobs. Best time to attack.

I breathe in deep. Time to face the fight.

To avoid walking through the Dark Forest, I teleport to the woodland mansion once I figure out its location numbers. Just like I did teleporting down here, though, I choose to land just a few blocks away from it. I pause, watching in the sunset for movement, bow poised and arrow held at the ready. But nothing moves.

I start climbing.

This close, the mansion feels bigger than I'd earlier thought. It reminds me of a church, with its deep-brown roof towering overhead. I run, finding new heights to climb, hoping I don't run into any mobs. I finally get to some land the same height as the canopy of the forest trees. From there, I climb onto one tree, jump to the next, and then the next, feeling like Tarzan. The forest feels so far below now.

Soon, I'm on top of the tree next to the mansion. I drop onto its roof, softly. I crawl up to the window and peek in.

The mansion's interior is lit with torches. And from where I stand, at the far corner, I can see the evoker.

I do a little jig in the back of my mind. I was right!

No one ever tells you how ugly-looking evokers are, in their gray skin and long black robes. This particular one is pacing the room, hands tucked into each sleeve of the robe, eyes wide and malicious. I slip away when it turns in my direction, hiding behind the wall next to the window.

The evoker wanders over to my window and peeks out. I hold my breath and stay hidden to the side, still and unmoving, until it goes away. I peek back into the room. The evoker's over at the far end now, looking out the opposite window. In the sky above, sunset will be waning soon, and night will come.

Now or never, Cece, I think.

I lean forward and smash the glass, nock my first arrow to the bow, and draw.

Everything after that happens so fast. First, a movement to my side catches my eye, one so quick and unexpected that the arrow leaves my bow completely out of surprise as I turn to discover the source of the movement. Luckily, my arrow strikes the evoker in the back.

Four Anarchians have suddenly climbed onto the roof.

The three boys and one girl are all dressed in wacky green camouflage, which I realize is designed to look like the dark forest. They must have blended in all this time, and I must have passed them on my way up and failed to notice them, since all name tags are hidden in this server. They must have then followed me up here.

Drat, I think.

But then I spot the fifth presence, the one all four of them seem to be fixated on: an orange-striped animal, standing right there on the roof with us. It's headed for me, blinking big tabby eyes.

"Cranky?" I say.

"Come here, you little—" one of the Anarchians starts, and leaps toward Cranky.

Out of nowhere, there is a *whoosh,* and six trap-like fangs appear on the roof. The Anarchian who has just come forward—one of the boys—sees it too late.

The trap snaps, gobbling him up in hungry teeth. He disappears in a *poof,* his inventory scattering all over the roof.

Then there is a growl, and the evoker leaps through the broken window and onto the roof.

CHAPTER TWELVE

THE EVOKER PLANTS THEMSELF BETWEEN all of us. On one side, Cranky and I. On the opposite side, the three remaining Anarchians.

The evoker lifts their arms. About them swirls glowing wind, a gathering of power.

Oh, nuts! I realize. It's going to release vexes!

So I do the only thing I know how to: I lift my bow, fully drawn, and fire.

The arrow strikes the evoker clean, but it's too late; they have already released four vexes.

Up close, the vexes are winged ghosts, if winged ghosts could hold iron swords, shriek like bats, and be always angry. They move even faster than the evoker, turning their attention toward the three Anarchians standing together.

"Drat!" another one of the boys says, then leaps away, chased out of view by two vexes. The other two vexes head for the remaining two Anarchians. The boy and the girl draw their weapons— a sword and an axe, both made of gold—and begin repelling them.

The evoker turns and faces Cranky and me.

I nock another arrow and draw, but the drawing time is agonizingly slow. If I fire, I'd hit it with a half-draw, which means it takes half the hit. So I hold my draw and wait for a full one.

The evoker moves faster than I expect as they raise their arms and send forward another set of fangs. I dodge to the side, but Cranky is doing what cats do best: getting in the way and preventing me from stepping into that spot. That suddenly turns out to be my saving grace, as a fang materializes out of nowhere and snaps shut, swallowing Cranky in its jaws.

"No!" I scream, but when the jaws disappear, the cat is still there, whole and unharmed. It *rawrs* at me.

Oh, right, I remember. *You take no damage.*

My bow is fully charged now. I raise it and fire at the evoker. The arrow misses.

Yikes! I think, right before the evoker raises their arms and releases another four vexes.

The vexes are fast, even faster than the evoker. I manage to hit one with a new, half-charged arrow, and two go off to fight the Anarchians. But the last one comes after me. I jump into the room through the broken window. It passes through the wall and chases me, as I try to nock a new arrow to my bow. I get the arrow in just in time to turn around and shoot as it descends on me, sword in hand. The arrow hits it and the vex screeches, falling toward my face, and then disappears in a cloud of smoke an inch from my nose.

Phew. Now, back to the roof.

I break another window and peek outside to see the three Anarchians on the roof, fighting off the vexes while darting and dodging the evoker's fangs. Whenever they get a chance, they pounce on the evoker as well. But no matter what they do, the evoker seems to avoid taking any damage from their hits, and just releases more vexes as it wishes.

So I take my time in my hiding place to draw my third arrow, slowly and steadily, and aim at the evoker. I release, and the arrow hits its target. I quickly draw another one for my last hit.

"Don't let her kill them!" one of the Anarchians says. "If she shoots that, she gets the Totem of Undying."

The what of what?

One of the boys—the same one who was earlier chased off the roof by a vex—peels away from the group and fires an arrow at me as he comes.

Out of nowhere, Cranky appears, flies across me, opens up its mouth wider than a cat ever should be allowed to, and swallows the arrow whole.

What the flying—

The boy is just as shocked as I am, but is quick to recover and nock another arrow. This one is not at full strength when it leaves his bow, but it's fast anyway.

The arrow is *this* close to my face when Cranky appears again, and this time I see it happen clearly. The cat isn't flying; the cat is glitch-teleporting. Yet again, Cranky zaps from wherever it once was and suddenly appears in the exact location of the arrow that's heading for me. It opens its mouth, so wide I can almost reach out and count its teeth, and swallows the arrow whole. The cat lands, looking unperturbed, and taking absolutely no damage. Instead, it just stands there and *rawrs* at me.

Between the surprise of being attacked and Cranky's swallowing arrows, I've completely forgotten about the evoker. Now that they have managed to occupy the other Anarchians with some fresh vexes, they turn back to me, still angry about my last arrow.

They raise their arms. Purple smoke swirls. Fangs appear out of the ground, and I'm too slow to make a move. One nips me in the foot. I feel the sting of taking damage, health down by a quick six hits.

Oh. It dawns on me now. Cranky protects me from *players* but not from mobs. Got it.

Only one thing left to do, then.

I draw my bow at full charge, arrow nocked, aim for the evoker, and release. The arrow hits the evoker full-on. First they shudder, then stagger, then drop down, blinking and blinking, until they're gone.

First Trial Completed! my chatbox announces, like a game-show host. **Congratulations!**

I stand there, elated but out of breath. *Did I just . . . complete the First Trial?*

"Look, the Totem of Undying!" one of the Anarchians—the girl—says, and then jumps at the object that has just appeared where the evoker once lay. But try as she might, she cannot pick it up.

"Okay, *what* is happening?" she says, turning her attention to me. "First this girl gets the Talisman of Chance, and now I can't pick up the Totem of Undying?" She takes two steps toward me. "Who are you?"

Talisman of Chance? Totem of Undying? What are these people talking about?

I take two steps back. "I—I—"

"Well, we'll just have to take it from her, huh?" the boy with the axe, fresh from killing off the rest of the vexes, says. He and the boy with the bow and arrow also advance on me.

"Yeah," Arrow Boy says. "We'll just have to wipe her off this server, and then we'll be free to take whatever we want."

They have circled me and Cranky: Arrow Boy and Axe Boy on either side, Sword Girl in front. They advance slowly, watching for any sudden movement from me.

"Let's make sure to hit her all at once," Sword Girl says. "The Talisman can't get them all."

"Maybe he won't, but I will," someone else says.

All our heads turn.

Standing on the edge of the roof is, to my astonishment, Were-Dragon. In her hand is a bow, fully drawn, and aimed at Arrow Boy, who is the closest to me.

"One more step, and you're gone," she says. "Turn around slowly and leave this mansion if you love yourself."

The three look at one another.

"We can take them," Arrow Boy says. "I take that one, you two take this—"

He doesn't even finish his sentence before the arrow leaves WereDragon's bow and sticks in him. He shudders, then disappears in a cloud, *poof!* His inventory scatters all over the roof. But even more important, so does his player head! All of us have eyes like wide saucers, but especially me. Apparently, this is what happens when players in this world defeat one another. Another one of the Ocury's weird mods. I wonder what my head looked like all the times I'd been killed by WereDragon.

"One shot!" Sword Girl exclaims, then takes two steps back, sheathing her sword. "That's a modded bow and an enchanted arrow!"

"You better believe it," WereDragon says, then nocks another arrow. "Anyone else have any bright ideas?"

"We're going, we're going," Sword Girl says, backing away slowly, as does Axe Boy. Once far enough, they turn their backs and jump off the roof, onto trees, and away.

WereDragon puts her bow and arrow away and turns to me. "We meet again, Cece." She gestures at the dropped item Sword Girl was trying to pick up. "You may claim your totem."

"Th—thank you," I manage to say, wondering why she has just saved me.

"You deserve it," she says. "And those three were just bullies. I hate bullies."

I shuffle over to where the totem has dropped, still dumbfounded by the whole experience. I pick it up, slowly.

Totem of Undying! says my chatbox.

"What is this totem thing?" I ask, holding it up and looking at it this way and that. It resembles a piece of wood with some precious stone embedded in it, but neither material feels recognizable.

"Oh, I forgot you're a noob," WereDragon says. "What you hold in your hand is basically another whole new life." She gestures toward Cranky, who's nuzzling at my feet. "Add that to your Talisman of Chance—"

"My what?" I look at where she's pointing. "Who, Cranky?"

"Cranky? You *named* him?"

"Yeah. 'Cos he's cranky all the time and going *rawr*." I look at the furry cat, who's simply sitting at my feet, minding his own business. "Talisman of Chance, huh. What does that even mean?"

"You have so much to learn," WereDragon says. "Come, let's leave this place. That evoker will soon be back."

"Like . . . respawn? I thought evokers don't—"

"This is Anarchia," WereDragon interrupts. "Nothing is normal."

Well, at least *that* part is true.

"I have a place," I say. "Underground. Not far from here. We can teleport there."

"Oh no, no, we can't," WereDragon says. "You've just completed the First Trial. And once you start completing the Haven Trials, it's goodbye to teleporting. From now on, it's you against the big, bad world of Anarchia, all on foot." She jumps off the roof and onto a tree. "Welcome to the Ocury's playground, quester. Best hurry along, now. Night's coming."

CHAPTER THIRTEEN

THE DARK FOREST IS MUCH smaller than I'd thought, and my underground base is much closer as a result. Our journey through is straightforward but not uneventful. We encounter a bunch of mobs going out—a few spiders, some zombies, some skeletons, one Enderman. WereDragon, it turns out, is quite skilled. She slices through them like a knife through butter. She layers hits together into combos and switches from melee to ranged and defense weaponry—sword, bow, shield—with ease. Some mobs don't even make it close to us before she's taken them out. They disappear in a chorus of *poofs*, leaving clouds in our wake. Without armor like hers, there is very little I have to do other than make sure I hide behind Cranky so no mobs easily get to me.

In no time, we clear the canopy and are back out in the grassland. Night is almost here. It takes me awhile to find the exact tree I'd built beneath, during which time WereDragon is forced to take out a creeper and two zombies. Once I find it, though, I quickly dig my way back to the stairs, and we're home free in no time.

"Not bad," WereDragon says, looking about at the room. "A waste of time, though, because we need to be out of here, like, yesterday."

"Why?"

"Because you will need to leave here soon and head back to the wastelands if you're going to complete the Second Trial."

"Right." I pause. "And that is?"

"Wither."

Though I can't tell, I'm pretty sure there must be a smile on her face as she says this, because of how stricken I become, how my whole body freezes at the word.

"A . . . Wither?"

"Well and truly alive," WereDragon says. "And worse, you're going to be the one to spawn it."

"I don't understand."

"Oh, you will, once you get there."

Another shiver runs down my spine. I don't know much about Withers, but the one thing I know is that they're the mobs with the most health in all of Minecraft. To defeat them means things like Strength potions and the most powerful weapons, none of which I have.

"Wow," I say, opening up the chest and gathering the rest of my stored resources. "Wow." I would sit down if I could.

"Are you all right?"

"No," I say. "No, I don't think I'm all right."

We stand there together in silence.

"Awk-ward," WereDragon says. "What's eating you?"

"I just—" I rummage through the remaining tools and re-sources, placing them each in my inventory. "I'm doing every-thing I need to, everything I *can* to get to my best friend. But

nothing is working like it should. Everything is just . . . too much."
I pause my raiding of the chest. "A *Wither*? I'm not sure I can do
it. What's even the point of trying? Maybe I should just give up."

WereDragon is silent, the first time she's not talking outside of
when we're slipping past mobs. No quips, no jokes—just silence.

Eventually, she says, "Well, I think you can do it."

I snap the chest closed. "Have you seen my inventory? Have
you seen my aim? I'm useless out there."

"If you've survived this long in Anarchia, then you're tougher
than you think."

"I don't know. I just—"

"Listen," WereDragon says. "Look on the bright side. You have
a Totem of Undying, which means fighting the Wither doesn't
actually mean sure death. At least even if your health drains, you
don't just die immediately—not unless you've used the totem already before then. Then there's your Talisman of Chance—"

"And what exactly does it *do*?" I ask, pointing at Cranky, who
is curled up in a corner, having followed us down here.

"*He* is one of the most powerful resources you can ever have in
this game," WereDragon says, stressing the "*he*." I didn't even
know Cranky was a *he*.

"How's that?"

"Because as long as the Talisman—Cranky—is with you, no
Anarchian can ever harm you. Ever." She motions toward him.
"Which, by the way, I have to ask. How did you get him to be loyal
and protect you?"

"Uhh, fed him a salmon?"

"And that's it?"

"That's it."

"Whoa. Do you know how long I've been searching for him?

From the day I dropped into this world, the legend of the glitchy cat that couldn't be modded out was everywhere. Every Anarchian has been on the lookout for him, but I've never met anyone who has been lucky enough to find him. Until now."

"More like he found me," I say, looking to the cat. "So he's not supposed to be a part of this world, then?"

"Nope," she says. "He was a passive mob that malfunctioned during the Ocury's meddling, and ended up protecting players instead. If an Anarchian is trying to attack you, he gets in the way, or swallows their weapons. The Ocury tried to write him out once, but I guess they couldn't so they just left him in here. But they managed to make it that he only protects one player at a time: his current owner. As long as the owner of the Talisman of Chance is still alive, he will protect them. The only way for someone to take him from his current owner—from you—will be to first physically remove him from where you are, somehow. That often means getting the owner killed by a mob or something, since the talisman won't let you do it yourself. Or, if you can lure or separate him from his owner long enough, you can try to gain his loyalty and trust. I'm guessing by feeding him, since that's how you did it."

"Wow." I look at Cranky anew, watch him lick himself in the corner, swishing a tail here and there. "So, he's like, not really supposed to be here or be like this, huh?"

"Not in the slightest."

I look back to her. "How long have *you* been here?"

The question takes her by surprise. "Awhile," she says, and I can feel the sigh in her words. "Long enough to complete the first two Haven Trials."

My eyes widen as much as they can. "You've defeated the Wither?"

"Yup," she says. "And even gotten to the Third Trial."

My eyes almost burst out of their sockets. "And what was there—at the Third Trial? What did you see?"

"Dunno. Died before I could find out whatever the mob boss was. Too many mobs in the very location you spawn, and I was all alone." She chooses a corner. "Let's reset our spawn points. Don't want to get killed and have to walk all the way back again."

"Wait, when did all this happen?"

She pauses. "Too long ago. I can't even remember."

"I don't understand," I say. "Why didn't you just go back?"

"*Because*," she says, her tone getting stronger, "it turns out that to get through to the Third Trial, you need help." She looks sad, saying this. "No matter how powerful or skilled you are, no matter how good your armor is—without friends to watch your back and help you fight off tons of mobs, it is impossible to cross to the Third Trial alone. And, I don't know if you've noticed, but making friends in Anarchia is kinda hard when everyone is trying to kill you."

I nod. "I see. Maybe I can be your friend then."

She looks at me. I can see her anticipation, waiting for me to withdraw the offer, to say, *Sike! You thought!* Almost like she'd never really had someone want to be her friend before.

"If you promise not to kill me again, that is," I say.

"Oh, I'm not killing you, don't worry," she says. "I have a rule, a personal code: no killing the same Anarchian more than three times."

"Oh," I say. "Why three times?"

"Magic number," she says. "But also because I just . . ." I can sense her negotiate another sigh. "I think everyone needs a personal code, you know? Of what you will do and what you won't do. In Anarchia, where anything goes, I want to be able to say I'm not like the Ocury, who has no limits. I want to be . . . fair."

There is some more silence between us.

"Join me on my quest," I say.

"What?"

"Help me get through the Second Trial, and I will go with you on the Third Trial. We'll complete the Haven Trials together."

"Like . . . a team?"

"Exactly," I say. "Or, maybe . . . friends?"

She stares at me again, with that same hesitation, unsure if I'm being for real or not.

"Let's take some time on it," she says, finally. "I'm going AFK in a while, but I'll reset my spawn point here so we can meet when next you log in. Let's see if you're still up for it then."

With that, she goes AFK. I go ahead and set my spawn point, hoping—*praying*—that she's still here when I return.

CHAPTER FOURTEEN

"WATCHU EATING?"

It was break time, and for the first time since starting at Gemshore Secondary, Cece was eating a packed lunch at the food court. Joachim dropped by, carrying his lunch of meat pies and a Coke.

"Club sandwiches," Cece said. "You want one?" She extended one of the cuts of bread and veggies held together with a toothpick toward him. He took it and munched.

"Mmm, okay!" he said nodding. "Fancy stuff. Tastes like it, too."

"My Iya—my mother, she makes them," Cece said. "When my friend Reesa used to come over on weekends"—she paused, catching herself—"my mother would make them for us. And we'd have them while we gamed."

Joachim nodded some more. "Minecraft?"

"Sorry?"

"The game you played—Minecraft?"

"Yeah."

He pointed to another one of the cut sandwiches. "Do you mind?"

Cece shrugged. He picked it up, placed it in his mouth, and closed his eyes. "So good."

Cece chuckled. "I see you like food."

"Oh, you have no idea," he said. "My grandmama says she wonders where all the food goes to in my body, because I'm always eating yet I'm still neither tall nor fat. I tell her I eat because I know where it goes—into the toilet." He slapped his mouth with a hand. "Oh, I shouldn't be talking about toilet at lunch." He slapped his other hand over his mouth.

Cece laughed. She hadn't found reason to laugh like this in a while.

"Maybe you should come by, then," she found herself saying.

He paused, regarding her. For a moment, he was the spitting image of WereDragon back in Anarchia, watching to see if she was truly offering something real or if it was all a joke.

"Iya says I should invite you over to the house, for lunch," Cece said. "That's what she was telling me in the car the other afternoon, when you were helping me with the map. So, if you want to come . . ." She shrugged.

"Okay," he said, nodding. "Sure."

"Is there any food in particular you like?" she asked. "I could tell her to make something."

He smiled, looking at his meat pie and Coke. "From what I've just eaten, I think I'll like whatever she makes."

The two ate some more in silence. After a while, Joachim asked: "How did it go? With your map thingy. Anarchia, right?"

"Yes, Anarchia," Cece said, and told him everything, giving him the rundown from building the base to finding and defeating the evoker and escaping with WereDragon and Cranky's help.

"Finding an ally in that kind of PvP land," Joachim said. "Sounds like a huge deal."

"It kind of is," Cece said. "She's going to help me complete the Second Trial. I'm going to spawn and then fight a Wither."

His eyes widened. "A *Wither!*"

"Yup."

"Wow, that's . . . brave. Must be a special friend if you're going to fight a Wither to get to her."

"Yeah, she is," Cece said, looking wistful. "Therese is the one person in this world who knows me, understands me."

Joachim munched on a meat pie and said, between chews, "You miss her?"

Cece had never really thought about it, exactly. Mostly, her focus had been on getting to Haven and being reunited. But now that she thought about it, so many of the things that she and Therese used to have were gone, Silver Oaks included. All that was left was simply . . . space, waiting to be filled by something else. Or someone else.

"I think so," she said finally, because she wasn't sure if it was Therese she missed, or simply having a best friend.

"Well, at least if you don't defeat the Wither, you still have friends," Joachim said.

"What friends?" asked Cece.

Joachim paused. "Oh, uh—"

"Oh, you mean you."

"And your Anarchian friend, maybe?"

Cece smiled wryly. "I guess?"

The bell for five minutes to the end of break rang. Joachim took up the rest of the meat pies and stuffed his face. Cece found herself laughing again.

PART THREE

THE
FRIENDSHIP
QUEST

CHAPTER FIFTEEN

IT WAS A SUNNY SATURDAY in Gemshore Estate, one of those where the heat rose off the street tarmac and concrete sidewalks in waves. The kids from the estate rode their bikes up and down the streets, their parents shouting warnings through doorways, asking them to put on sunscreen. Cece watched the afternoon with interest through the kitchen window of the Alao house, standing on a short stool next to her mother.

"Come help me slice the plantains," Iya said, motioning to the yellowing fruits on the counter. Cece heaved a long sigh and picked up the small, safer knife her mother always reserved for her.

"What's that?" Iya said, and chuckled. "Sighing like an old woman again." She looked over from chopping peppers. "Is it Therese?"

Cece shrugged. "Maybe."

"Dearie, I thought you were already making new friends? Isn't that why Joachim—Jo, right?—isn't that why he's coming over for lunch today?"

"Yes, but—" Cece sliced off the top of the first plantain and ran a knife down the length of it so she could peel all the skin in one fell swoop.

"On a day like this, right?" she continued. "We'd be outside, biking like everyone else. Or maybe inside, gaming. But she's not here, so I'm here instead, peeling plantains."

"But you're spending quality time with your dear old mama," Iya said. "You don't think that's a fair trade?"

"I see you every day, Iya."

Her mother laughed. "Fair. Boring as it might seem to you, though, I still prefer it to you burying your face in a screen all day, or worse, immersing yourself in that game, getting lost in a world of zeros and ones."

"It's Minecraft, not zeros and ones," Cece said. "Plus, we do the same thing in there that we'd have done outside anyway, which is just hang out and have fun."

"Well, today, you get to both hang out with a new friend and have fun, whether inside or outside. Though I'd rather the latter than the former."

Her mother finished with the peppers and moved on to chopping up the other vegetables for the fried rice she was cooking—green beans, onions, carrots. Cece peeled the remaining plantains, sliced them at the angles her mother liked, then salted them lightly in preparation for the frying. Iya took over at this point, though, because she did not like Cece handling hot oil.

Baba came through the front door.

"Look who I found lurking near the gate outside," he said, giving way to reveal a sheepish Joachim, who waved weakly. Cece waved back.

"Some of the kids were picking on him," Baba was saying

in a low voice. "Saying mean things about what he was wearing."

Cece looked over at Joachim, and suddenly could see why. The kids at Gemshore Estate were the kind who did not take kindly to children from outside the estate, and called them mean names whenever they could. Joachim did indeed look like many kids from outside the estate—well-dressed, but not wearing many imported items, especially sneakers and shirts. Nor did the kids from outside wear cool watches or hair accessories. Joachim himself wore handmade slippers, which actually looked pretty cool, but were a dead giveaway in Gemshore.

"Oh dear, we're so sorry about that!" Iya said, waving him back into the living room. "Sit—let's get you a drink. Whew, look at you sweating like that!" She signaled to Cece with her eyes, urging her to ask him what he wanted to drink.

"What would you like?" Cece asked. "We have soda and fruit juice."

"Just . . . water," Joachim said shyly. Cece went to get it.

"How come your parents didn't wait after dropping you off?" Baba asked. "We would've loved to meet them."

"I didn't get . . . dropped off," Joachim said. "I took a bus."

Gasps went about the room, but Cece was most intrigued by this information.

"Your parents let you take public transport *alone*?" Baba asked.

"Well, my granny does," Joachim said, receiving the tall glass of water from Cece and gulping it down.

"And what do your parents have to say about that?" Iya asked.

"Well—they . . . um . . ." He scratched the back of his head. "I don't know what they think. I haven't seen them in a long time."

"Oh," Iya and Baba said together, glancing at each other.

"Yeah," Joachim said. "I've always lived with my granny. But she doesn't drive, so I've always had to go everywhere I need to by bus. She used to go everywhere with me, back when she was stronger. Now, she says I'm old enough."

"You see!" Cece was saying. "If he's old enough, I'm old enough, too."

"Shh, dearie," Iya said. "Jo is trying to tell us something important."

"Oh no, it's nothing important," Joachim said. "Just my everyday life."

The conversation after that was stilted and awkward, so much so that Iya agreed it was okay for them both to go outside and play until lunch was ready. Cece took Joachim down to the garage to get her bike. She had a newer one in addition to an older one that got damaged and was later repaired. She offered him the second bike.

"Oh, I can't ride a bike," he said, sheepish again.

"Oh?" Cece said. "Why not?"

Joachim leaned over and touched the bell of the bike, ringing it with a loud *ping!*

"I've just never had one," he said. "Or access to one."

"Come, then," Cece said. "It's easy. I'll teach you."

So they went out into the street, and Cece showed him how to put his feet on the pedals and balance on the bike. She showed him which one was the hard brake and which was the soft, and how turning the handlebars allowed him to choose direction.

Joachim failed at pretty much all of it.

It didn't help that, soon enough, the kids of Gemshore showed up, running along with them and singing and chanting mockingly as Cece pushed him up and down the street.

"Hakuna, Matata, he can't stay on two tires.

"Hakuna, Matata, he'll try and try and try-er."

On and on and on they went, causing Cece to get so fed up that she suggested they quit riding and put the bicycle back in the garage. Joachim seemed like he didn't mind going on despite the chants, but Cece was so upset by them that he agreed, although he looked sad about it. Cece then felt bad herself and wondered if she should've just let him do what he wanted.

Lunch, after Iya had called them back in, was quiet and fidgety. Cece's parents asked them both what had happened out there, but neither of them spoke about it. Once lunch was done, Baba asked if they were going to hang out indoors and play some video games.

"I think I'm just going to go," Joachim said, looking crestfallen, though he managed a smile.

"Oh?" Iya said. "Are you sure you're okay, dear? Sure you don't want us to give you a ride home?"

"I'll be fine," he said. "I only know the bus route anyway, which won't be very good for driving."

Cece went to open the gate for him. "I'm sorry," she said as she let him out.

He smiled his small smile. "At least you tried," he said, then left.

Back inside, Cece's parents hugged her, mumbling their concern for Joachim. Cece simply wished she could store this hug in her bag, take it to school, and hand it to him. That way, he, too, could feel the warmth of always having people around who cared about him.

CHAPTER SIXTEEN

BACK AT SCHOOL ON MONDAY, Cece still felt bad for Joachim. All through the morning, she noticed he was quieter than usual, not speaking up much in class.

During break time, Joachim sat alone, not going out for lunch as usual. Cece decided she was going to cheer him up. She had packed a lunch—the club sandwiches he'd enjoyed. So she went out and used some of her saved lunch money and bought two fruit juices. They could share her club sandwiches and drink juices and talk about Minecraft if he wanted.

When she came back, Joachim was surrounded by three classmates, all girls. The leader was someone she recognized—the backbencher girl named Ofure whom she had met on the first day.

"So, you think because you're a teacher's pet, you won't answer when we talk to you?" Ofure was saying.

"Go away, Ofure, please, I don't have time today" was Joachim's response.

"And what if I don't?" Ofure said, edging closer. "What if I stand right here and don't go away? You'll report me to a teacher or what?"

"No, I'll just leave," Joachim said, and rose, but the girl put a hand on his shoulder and pushed him back down.

"I'm not finished," she said. "Where do you think you're going when I'm not finished?"

"Leave him alone."

The words were out of Cece's lips so quickly, she couldn't believe she had said them. Then she realized why this scene seemed so familiar to her, and why she had responded the way she did.

It was like WereDragon saving her from the Anarchians on the roof of the woodland mansion.

"What did you say?" Ofure asked, turning to face her.

"I said leave him alone." Cece paid the girl even less attention now, tossing the cold bottles of locally made hibiscus juice from hand to hand. She opened the caps of each, hoping to pass one to Joachim and to relieve the coldness deadening her palm. The deep redness of a few drips of juice ran down her fingers like sweet blood.

Ofure stepped up and faced Cece. "And what if I don't?"

"Why are you always looking for trouble?" Cece found herself saying. "Why don't you backbenchers just mind your business?"

"You *what?*" Ofure said, aghast. "Who are you calling a backbencher?"

Then she slapped Cece's hand.

It all happened so fast. One moment, Cece was holding two bottles. Next, they were on the ground.

But between those two moments, her hands had reflexively responded to the anticipation of the slap and pressed the bottles.

Deep-red juice jumped out and splattered all over Ofure: hair, face, uniform.

Everyone froze, mouths opened into a big round O.

"Oh, my—" Cece started.

"Pfft!" Ofure spluttered. "What . . . what . . ."

And then she screamed.

Cece's ears were still ringing when Ofure stopped. The girl looked at her clothes, then back at Cece.

"Look at my uniform!" she screamed, pointing. "Look at it!"

But just when she leaned forward, arm raised in attack and Cece flinching in anticipation of the hit, a voice boomed from the balcony above them:

"Joachim!"

Everyone looked up. It was the math teacher, Mr. Gbenga.

"What is going on here?" the man said, then pointed at Ofure. "Why does your uniform look like that? Is that what we teach you about neatness in this school?"

"I did not—"

"Hush," he said. "Come up here. If you cannot stay neat for a whole day, maybe you should be stuck with the teachers in the staff room. That'll teach you to be neat." He looked at the other two girls, Ofure's friends, who had stood to the side this whole time, watching the event unfold with a little hint of amusement. "And you two, be on your way!"

The three girls dispersed, Ofure heading for the stairwell to meet Mr. Gbenga upstairs in the staff room. She turned about and gave Cece a threatening look.

Oops, thought Cece. *If I wasn't in trouble before, I'm in trouble now.*

"Are you okay, Joachim?" Mr. Gbenga was saying.

"Yes sir," Joachim said. "They were bothering me. But Cece came to my rescue."

Mr. Gbenga looked at her, and she suddenly felt very small.

"Well, that's good, looking out for your friends like that," he said, then extended a warning finger. "Stay out of trouble, you two, all right?" With that, he turned and left.

"'Rescue'?" Cece said, wiping the few drops of hibiscus juice that had splashed on her uniform. "I'm not sure that's what I did."

"Maybe not," Joachim said, and smiled. "But he's right that friends look out for each other, and you did look out for me, so . . ."

"And I should've done that with the estate kids, too," Cece said. "I should have spoken up. If friends protect each other, then I should not have kept quiet that whole time. I'm sorry."

"It's okay," he said. "So that means we're . . . friends?"

Cece shrugged. "I guess so?"

"Yeah, I guess so," Joachim echoed.

"Cool," Cece said, then held out her ziplock bag of club sandwiches. "Here. I was going to give you these with one of those drinks before Ofure happened. But now, maybe . . . peace offering?"

Joachim grinned, then the grin widened into a smile as he took the bag. "You know I can never resist a good club sandwich."

When I wake up in my underground base, WereDragon is nowhere to be found. Cranky, however, is still in the corner, curled into himself. He offers me a small *rawr* of welcome.

"Thank you," I say. "Any idea where our new friend is?"

Rawr is his response.

"I guess you're only useful for swallowing weapons, then."

I take out the map and look through it. The Second Trial, it seems, is located deep in the heart of the desert wastelands. If we must go all the way over there from all the way over here, it means more than one to two days of travel. Unless I can defeat all the mobs I meet and build two underground bunkers to spend the night, there's no way I'm making this journey without dying.

"At least I have the Totem of Undying," I say to myself.

"Doesn't stop you from dying, though," WereDragon says.

I spin around, startled. She is coming down the stairs, into the room.

"I went back to the mansion to get some resources for the trip," she said.

"Oh," I say. "What were you saying about the Totem of Undying?"

"That that's not how it works," she says. "Doesn't give you another life, per se. You just don't get to die immediately if you take a huge life-draining damage. Which is good for the Second Trial, because the Wither has something called the Wither effect? If that hits you once, you're gone. But with your totem, you should be able to stay alive to keep fighting."

She begins to drop some items on the floor. "These are for you. I'm not allowed to help you in the actual fight against the Wither, so I'm just going to prepare you instead."

It's mostly food and a lot of raw iron. There's also a bunch of cobblestone blocks.

"What am I going to do with all these?" I ask, picking them up.

"Level up, to start," she says. "You'll need to upgrade from your stone to iron if you're going to survive out there."

With her help, I locate everything I need in my inventory's

recipe book. I use the cobblestone to craft a quick furnace, then place all the iron in it, with coal as fuel. After a bit of a wait, I get some iron ingots. Then, I follow the recipe book's guides on how to craft the iron armor I need: helmet, chestplate, leggings, boots. I fill my four armor slots with them. Next, we do weapons and tools: a sword and a pickaxe. Afterward, my inventory moves up to:

- 6 iron ingots
- 9 cobblestone blocks
- 1 iron sword
- 1 iron pickaxe

"Would've loved diamond for these," WereDragon says. "But apparently there's no diamond on Anarchia."

"No diamond *at all*? How did you get yours, then?"

"Off some other Anarchians," she says. "I have no idea where they get them. Trust me, I've tried, and have found nothing. They must have some arrangement with the Ocury or something."

She drops some more items in front of me and I pick them up:

- 1 Potion of Fire Resistance
- 1 Potion of Regeneration

"Now, those two you will definitely need for fighting the Wither. Make sure you don't die and lose them."

"Where did you get them?" I ask, tucking them away.

"Fought a witch," she says.

"There are witches in Anarchia?" I ask worriedly.

"Yup," she says. "Prepare for anything, and you'll never be surprised. Even by witches."

She checks that I have all I need, then asks me to pack up everything else, including the crafting table and torches. We leave one to prevent any hostile mobs from spawning here. When I'm about to pack up the chests, I realize my inventory is full and can't contain them.

"We'll make another one," she says. "We'll have to keep making new housing every night or two, anyway."

"Thank you," I say. "For helping and protecting me. For being a . . . friend?"

"You mean 'ally,'" she corrects. "Not so sure about 'friend' yet."

"But that's what friends do, right? Not just hang out, right? They help and protect each other?"

"Well, going by that, I'd say you have none."

"Oof," I say. "Harsh much?"

"Think about it," she says. "If you have friends, why aren't they helping you on this quest?" She pauses. "Oh, that's right. Because you're actually on this quest because of this . . . friend? Same one who just dumped you here to fend for yourself?"

"She would've helped if she could," I say. "We're just unable to reach each other right now."

"Or maybe she just doesn't care," WereDragon says.

"How can you say that?" I am aghast. "That is simply not true."

"Maybe you're right," she concedes. "Maybe she's trying her best to get to you as much as you are trying to get to her. Or maybe—just maybe—friends are overrated."

"I see you're a windower." The words are out of my lips before I can hold them back.

"A what?"

"You know—like a neutral mob, you leave things alone as long as they do you. But once they come too close, you fight back to push them away."

It was WereDragon's turn to say, "Ouch."

"Sorry, I didn't mean to put it like that," I say quickly. "It's just . . ." My mother's words come back to me now. "Friendship can be difficult sometimes, you know? But you have to work through the hard times to make it better."

"And what if the hard times never end? What if I always have to be a windower because it's the only way I can win?"

"Then maybe it's not really about winning? Maybe just the fun, the experience is enough?"

WereDragon laughs. "You should tell that to the Wither when we get there."

With that, she starts back up the stairs. Cranky watches her go, as do I. When I turn to him, he gives me one of his trademark *rawrs*.

"Don't blame me," I say. "Sometimes, the only thing we can do is follow." I follow WereDragon up the stairs, beckoning him. "Come on, boy. We have a Trial to complete."

CHAPTER SEVENTEEN

"ALL RIGHT, LISTEN," WEREDRAGON SAYS. "We're going to find the materials to build a Wither."

"I'm sorry—what?" I ask, incredulous.

"We're going to find the materials," she repeats. "But *you* are going to build a Wither. If someone else spawns it and we fight and defeat it, the victory goes to that person's name. It has to be you."

We've begun the trip toward our first point of reference on my map: the place marked *Second Trial*. According to WereDragon, who it turns out knows every nook and cranny of Anarchia like the back of her hand, this is not the location of the Wither itself, but instead three Wither skulls. According to her explanation, these skulls and four blocks of soul sand are the items we'll need to build and spawn a Wither. After which we must then kill it.

"How come I get to hear this part last?" I query. "Also, are you saying the Ocury wants *me* to build a monster and fight it just to complete a Trial?"

"Not just that," she says. "When you kill the Wither, it drops a Nether star. You take that star into the mountains, and place it on an already built beacon. It's that beacon that transports us to the Third Trial. There's no other way to get there without doing that."

"Creeper!" I call out, as a creeper comes close to us. We're walking in the night, moving forward inch by inch and avoiding as many mobs as we can. But sometimes, a few find us, and we have no choice but to defend ourselves.

We jump out of the way as the creeper charges up, hisses, then explodes. Cranky is within its vicinity, but does not get hurt. He only makes a *rawr* and waits for us to continue.

We've spent two days on the road, moving past the woodland mansion and its forest and wandering back into grassland. We've yet to return to the village, though. WereDragon says it's not called the *"hunting ground"* for nothing, since that's where many of the rogue Anarchians tend to congregate. She tells me I was exceptionally lucky to not have happened upon a band of them there.

"If we're going to stay alive on this journey," she said, "we'll be better off running into an Enderman than an Anarchian."

We've been on the road for days, so we decide to stop to rest and reset our respawn points. The grassland is open, with no trees, so our best bet is an underground base. WereDragon sticks a few torches around. "Prevents mobs from spawning right next to us," she says. Then she pulls out an iron shovel and digs quickly, while I stand guard, praying silently that no mob comes close.

Of course, that prayer goes unanswered, and I have to fight off two zombies, a spider, and a skeleton who wander our way before WereDragon is done digging. Soon, though, she is underground with a torch lit, and calls on me to follow. Cranky comes in, then we close up our lair.

"All right," she says. "We need to strategize and hit the next sunset."

There's little time for chat. We go right to setting spawn points, with the only sounds about us those of a zombie or two groaning aboveground. The sweet droop of the spawn point reset action encircles us, the ticks pass, and then it's another night over as we reemerge to the low light of sunset. Or, as I've grown fond of calling it, *light-dark.*

"All right, our plan is in three stages," she says. "First: get the three Wither skulls. Depending on whether the place where the skulls are is empty or not, that could be the easy part."

"What's the place like? Where the skulls are?"

"At the bottom of an oasis lake," she says.

"Wha—ugh. Can this place get any more difficult?"

"Which brings us to the second stage of this plan: find some soul sand."

"Is that also here? In Anarchia? I thought you find that in the Nether?"

"Yes," she says. "But luckily for us, the Ocury has modded the Nether out of this world. So the good news is this: we can find soul sand in a small cavern called Soul Sand Valley that they have modded in here. Bad news: it's filled with lava and tons of mobs."

"Great."

"That's just stage two. Stage three: we have to find an appropriate place to spawn the Wither and then fight it."

"We can't just fight it out here in the open desert?"

"Sure we can. But only if you want to die."

"Oh."

"Yes. The best kind of place is some sort of underground mine in a stone mountain. And I know just one such place, up there in the mountains. The one time I fought the Wither and won, I did it there."

"Oh."

"And even better, once we win, the journey to the beacon will be short. No need to waste time crossing the desert again."

We open up the ground above us. The torches are still going. WereDragon packs them up and our little bubble of light vanishes.

We continue like this for four more days, crossing the grassland into the desert wastelands. The terrain moves from flat into dunes, which go higher and higher. The trees and grass disappear, and the few cacti we spot every now and then are the only green left for long distances. Every two days, we build a new underground rest stop, cook some new food for the next phase of the trip, refill our hunger bars, and reset our spawn points.

On the fifth day, we hit the oasis.

"Get down, get down," WereDragon says.

"What, what?" I ask, crouching. "It's still sunset—mobs aren't out yet."

"Yes, but Anarchians are," she says.

I look to the lake, where she's trained her focus, and see the people she's referring to. They're a bunch of Anarchians, all wearing diamond armor and one of them wearing a multicolored head. I wonder if he got it from another player after defeating them, just like when Arrow Boy's head fell off on that roof of the evoker's mansion. Looks like he's wearing the head just like any other collectible. They're tucked behind a nearby sand formation, which looks less and less natural the longer I look at it. It looks like they built it just so they wouldn't be easily spotted until the last second by anyone approaching the lake.

"Those are not just any Anarchians," WereDragon says. "That's Declan's crew."

"Who's Declan?"

"That one," she says, pointing to the one with the colorful head. "He's one of the meanest Anarchians you'll ever meet."

"Are they trying to get the Wither skulls, too?"

"No, they're just like me. They've beaten both the evoker and Wither and should be able to get into the Third Trial now. But for some reason I'm not sure of, they aren't trying to. Instead, they just hang around the locations of the Trials because they know vulnerable newbies will unknowingly show up. Then they attack them. That's how they rack up XP."

"What do they need XP for? Are they trying to become the Ocury like you are?"

"Maybe? I don't know. They can do some weird things in this place that most of us can't do. Like, they can still teleport, even *after* completing the Trials. Many Anarchians think they're in cahoots with the Ocury. They think the Ocury uses them as just one more obstacle to prevent us from completing the Trials." She sounds exasperated saying this. I can tell she doesn't like Declan and his crew very much.

"Anyway, I've run into them a bunch of times and managed to get away. So Declan is now always out for me, fighting me whenever we meet and hunting me whenever he can. I've avoided him and his crew since the last time, though. If it's just Declan by himself, I can take him. But his crew has grown much larger since then. With all their diamond armor, I'm sure I won't survive them as a pack."

"Wow," I say. "Best we hide, then."

"Best we hide."

We creep around our dune, ensuring that its shadow and the fading light keep us obscured. This does just enough of the work for a while, but soon, we're too close to the pack. Any more movement and we'll run into them.

"We'll have to wait them out," WereDragon says.

"Underground base?"

"You know it. Otherwise, they'll just spot us later."

We switch roles this time: I dig, she stands guard. Once we're done, we're about to go underground when I notice Cranky is nowhere to be found.

"Where's Cranky?" I ask. We look around, and for the life of us, can't find the cat.

"We have to go look for him," I say.

"No," says WereDragon. "He can fend for himself. Remember he doesn't take any damage."

"But what if someone else finds him and gets him to be loyal to them?"

"Tough luck, then," she says. "Should've fed him more often." She goes underground. "Quick, let's hide."

I poke my head above ground and look around for one last unsuccessful peek. Cranky is missing.

WereDragon has the thankless job of poking her head above the surface to watch for when the group of Anarchians leave. They take an awfully long time to do that, while I pace around our base, freaking out over what might have happened to Cranky. I'm not even bothered that now that I've lost him, I can be attacked by fellow players. I know Cranky barely said anything, but his presence was comforting, and I liked the idea of being responsible for someone other than myself.

"They're gone," WereDragon says. "We should move fast. They could be back."

"Then we'll go look for Cranky after?"

"You need to forget that cat and focus on what's important here," WereDragon says. "We need to complete this Second Trial and cross into the Third Trial."

We climb back to the surface and find the lake now deserted. Sunset is almost over, and mobs will spawn soon, so we creep as quickly as we can across the sand, and once we're by the lake, we dive into it.

Below, the lake is full of seaweed. Our movement is slowed down by the water. A squid swims past us, wiggling its tentacles. I remember not to freak out, because squids are passive mobs. But I also remember that even though most mobs can't swim, the drowned—underwater zombies—absolutely can. If night meets us down here, we will not be able to escape the drowned that will spawn underwater.

"The skulls are equally spaced in marked blocks," WereDragon is telling me, words bubbling underwater. "Start at that end and I'll start over here. Look for a block marked with a dark tree-like vein. If you find one and look closer, you'll see the black skeleton head frozen inside it."

I look around halfheartedly, my mind split between Cranky's unknown fate and the quest. But soon enough, I spot one of the blocks WereDragon's talking about. True to her word, it's a black block with vein-like decorations, but the eyes of the skeleton are there, its sockets wide open. I shriek in surprise when I find it, the shriek coming out in bubbles. But after a second, I get over that initial fear.

"Found one," I say, and start mining it with my hand.

"No," she says. "You have to mine it with an iron pickaxe or it won't drop." Then she starts swimming up. "Come, we need to catch our breath first, so we have enough time to finish it."

So, up we swim, back to the surface.

There's someone up there once we arrive, dressed in full diamond armor, wearing a colorful head. He looks like he's returned only to pick up a forgotten shield, but as soon as we come out of the water, he turns around and spots us.

"Well well well, WereDragon," says Declan. "We meet again." As he says this, I notice he is holding a lead in his hand. And at the other end, the lead tied around his neck, is Cranky.

Declan sticks a fence post in the ground and ties Cranky to it.

Rawr, says the cat.

Then Declan draws his sword and charges us.

CHAPTER EIGHTEEN

THE LAST TIME I GOT attacked by an Anarchian, there was at least a delay, a moment in which I could react. But this time, everything happens so fast.

Declan swings his sword and knocks me back into the water.

I plunge below the surface, the searing weight of damage taken and water threatening to pull me down. Diamond swords hit differently, and my damage stats tell me that I was lucky to have fallen into the water, out of sight. Otherwise, one more hit and that would've been my whole health gone.

I swim back to the surface as fast as I can. I jump out quickly enough to see Declan and WereDragon going at it, pulling out swords and shields as quickly as they can to parry each other's blows. They're fast, darting and coming together in melees, swords striking each other's armor. They look equally matched and like they'll be going at it for a while.

Then off to the side, I see Cranky, still tied to the post, unable to leave. I realize, now, that because it's in the programming of

passive mobs like him—cats, horses, and the like—to follow anyone who leashes them, he cannot follow me. He clearly did not
protect me from Declan's attack just now, so that programming
superseded his glitch.

Is there no end to the surprises in this forsaken world? I think.

I have to get him off that lead and back to protecting me. But
WereDragon's voice is firm in my head: *Remember what we came
here for.*

"I'll be back for you, Cranky," I say. Then I go against my better judgment and dive back into the lake.

Luckily, I still have my iron pickaxe. I pull it out and begin
digging at the first block. I have to dig for quite a while, slowly
running out of air, before the Wither skeleton skull pops out. It's
a large, black, ugly thing, and terrifies me even as I put it into my
inventory.

I swim back up to the surface. Declan and WereDragon are
still going at it; I can hear their grunts all the way over here.

I catch my breath and go back in again. The second skull
block is just as WereDragon had said, not far from the first. I start
mining it, too, and when it drops, I place it in my inventory. I go
up for my final breath of air, and soon realize that sunset has
turned into night, and it's time for mobs to start spawning.

Better be quick, I say to myself, and dive back in . . .

. . . and run into a newly spawned drowned.

The drowned is too close for me to draw out my sword. I guess
I catch it by surprise, too, because it gurgles and whacks me immediately. I'm knocked back by the force, but only a little because the water prevents it. My body goes into a minor convulsion,
warning me of my severely depreciating health. One more hit and
I'll be gone, game over.

Luckily, I switch pickaxe for sword quickly enough to deal with the drowned before it's able to get another hit in on me. After that, finding the third skull block goes much more quickly, maybe because I have no choice. I mine it as fast as I can, aware that another mob can spawn nearby. Then I head for the surface.

There are mobs everywhere when I come out of the lake.

I haven't seen this many hostile mobs in one place since the day I landed in Anarchia. It seems the desert has the most of them, because they're *everywhere*. Spiders, skeletons, creepers, Endermen, zombies. Declan and WereDragon are no longer fighting each other, but fighting off the mobs that have zeroed in on them. WereDragon seems to have it tougher, because she seems to be fighting a mob I haven't seen before: one throwing potions at her—a witch!

Luckily, there are few to no mobs around the lake, which gives me the little slice of time I need to get out of here.

I run toward Cranky and take off the lead at once. It drops for me as an item, but I don't even have time to pick it up.

Come, quick! I scream at him in my head as we run. Somehow, he hears me and comes along, as the spiders hiss and the zombies groan and everything converges on us.

Then Declan, who has finished fighting off the last of his mobs, turns toward me, and fires an arrow.

But just like last time, Cranky, at last free, jumps up and swallows it.

Declan, unlike the Anarchians at the woodland mansion, does not waste any more arrows on me. He looks at me, then at WereDragon—who's still fighting off the witch—and says:

"Until next time, suckers."

Then he runs off, his colorful patchwork head disappearing into the dark.

"Come, come!" I scream at WereDragon, who has just managed to finally dispatch the witch and is picking up the potions the witch has dropped. The mobs—many now, and almost doubled in number from last time—are almost on us.

"To the hideout!" WereDragon screams in reply, and all of us—me, her, Cranky—bound toward the dune that last hid us. We have to dodge a couple of the newly spawning mobs, but we stay safe. My health regenerates—not quickly enough for my taste, but enough that I won't die just yet.

We soon arrive at the dune and our underground hideout.

"In, in!" I say, and goad Cranky down. I jump in after him. WereDragon, who is bringing up the rear, is a few steps out.

"Come on!" I say, then pull out my bow, draw, and aim at the spider on her heels, right behind her.

If my aim is true one time, I think, recalling all the cool archers I'd read about in fantasy novels, *let it be this one time*.

I let go.

The arrow catches the spider dead-on. It doesn't kill it, but sets it back enough that some space opens up between it and WereDragon, giving her time to make it to the opening, where I stand.

She jumps in at the last second, and I pull out a sand block and seal us all underground.

"Nice shot!" says WereDragon, once we're back safe in the hideout.

"Was it?" I ask, though my head feels like it wants to explode at the praise. "Eh, it's just whatever."

"No it wasn't 'whatever,'" she says. "You literally saved my butt out there." She pauses. "Thanks."

"It's cool," I say. "You've saved *my* butt many times before, so."

"Haha, true," she says, then looks at me. "You're not a bad ally to have, though."

I let the warm feeling of that go through me as I return to Cranky and give him a pat.

"Do you have any fish?" I ask WereDragon. "Salmon or cod?"

"None," she says. "But I have a fishing rod, so we can get some from the lake tomorrow. That's if Declan and his crew don't show up and surround it again."

"Will that be too late? Tomorrow?"

She looks at Cranky. "Nah. I saw that he protected you from Declan, so I figure he's still got some juice until tomorrow."

Cranky says *Rawr* to her in response.

"You're welcome," she says to him.

I chuckle inside at their exchange, and then start to prepare to reset my spawn point, but WereDragon stops me.

"No need yet," she says. "We're going back soon."

"Right," I say. "What do we do then?"

"We wait," she says. "The mobs hanging around will wander away eventually, especially as they can't see us. Then we'll go back to the lake and get the skulls."

"Oh, that," I say. "I've already collected them." I drop them for her to see.

"Oh," she says. "That was . . . wise." She looks at me again. "You're a *really* not-bad ally."

"Some people would call that a 'friend,'" I say. "But what do I know."

"Haha," she says.

"I don't think I've seen you laugh before," I tell her.

"Well," she says. "Anarchia doesn't really give you much to laugh about."

"True," I say. "But we can laugh, the two of us. If you want, I can tell jokes."

Now she laughs even harder and longer, a *"hahahaha."*

"You don't sound like someone who makes a lot of jokes, Cece."

This is the first time she's used my name, and it feels intimate. I smile inside, and suddenly realize that between her and Joachim, all my negative feelings about Therese are gone. *Does making new friends make someone feel better about old or lost ones?* I wonder.

A zombie groans and interrupts the silence.

"That seems like the last of them," WereDragon says. "Listen."

We listen. There are no more groans.

"Time to get some rest," she says. "I'm going AFK for a while, so I'll reset my spawn point here. You should be doing so, too. Tomorrow, we head for the Soul Sand Valley."

"Oh. I might be awhile coming back here, to Anarchia," I say. "I have . . . some stuff to attend to. You know, IRL."

"Oh," she says, then seems to take some time to ponder her options. "Do you want me to wait for you?"

"Do you want to?" I ask.

"I guess," she says. "I can't get to the Third Trial without you anyway, so."

"Okay," I say. "What about we return here at a particular time every meatspace day or two? We could agree on something that'll be good for us."

"Okay," she says. "But we'll have to agree on that in the . . . meatspace."

"Right," I say. "Maybe I can send you a message?"

"I don't have a phone."

"Oh. How are you playing this again?"

"Console," she says.

"Okay. So just like me, then. Maybe I can friend you and message you there."

"Okay," she says. "Sorry, I'm not, like, really good at the making-friends stuff. Plus, my parents are very strict about exchanging information with strangers online."

"Mine, too," I say. "Don't worry, I completely understand."

"Okay," she says. "I'll send you a message. Add me, and then we'll decide."

"Okay," I say. "Good night, WereDragon."

She's silent for a moment, before she says: "Aminata."

"Sorry?"

"Aminata," she repeats. "You can call me that. It's my IRL name."

"Aminata," I say. "Good night and see you on the other side."

CHAPTER NINETEEN

FOR THE FIRST MORNING SINCE she'd started Gemshore Secondary, Cece was smiling on her way into school.

"Oooh, look at you glowing," Iya said, as they drove the short distance to the school. "Did something happen?"

"Not really," Cece said. "Just . . . I think I'm doing okay now. Better."

"With what?"

"Everything?" Cece replied. "I said sorry to Jo at school and we're cool again. He isn't sad or angry about . . . you know, the whole disaster lunch. And then, I'm no longer sad about Therese. Not like before, anyway."

"Oh?" said Iya.

"Yeah. I'm going to speak to her soon anyway."

"How so? I don't think Mr. Njinga has sent across a new phone num—"

"No, I mean through Minecraft. I'll soon see her there."

"Oh, right. I forgot you people can chat within that game of yours." Iya looked across at her daughter and smiled. "Well, whatever makes you happy, I'm happy with. Especially when it means you have friends you like and are good with. Just as long as you're not meeting random, dangerous people while in that game."

Cece thought of WereDragon—*Aminata*—and shook her head. "No dangerous people there. Just friends."

Iya dropped her off, and on her way inside, she ran into Joachim. He high-fived her by way of greeting.

"Are you always this happy?" Cece asked. "Except when you're not, like the other day."

"Kinda," Joachim said, grinning.

"Because?"

He shrugged. "I dunno. Always just been this way."

Cece thought that maybe she needed more of this kind of freewheeling happiness. She had just started to feel some of it in her life now, and she liked the way it felt.

First two periods were math, a period-subject pairing she absolutely hated. But instead of scowling through it as she often did, she found herself coasting, listening to Mr. Gbenga talk and talk. Next two periods before break time was social studies, and as bulky as the notes she had to take were, she didn't feel cranky about it, either.

During break time, she and Jo sat in what was becoming their usual spot in the food court. She shared her club sandwiches with him and he shared his Coke with her.

"So, what's been happening in your deathland of Anarchia?"

Cece laughed. "It's not deathland—we barely die there. There're a ton of hostile mobs, though. Hostile players, too. Had to fight one off just the other day."

"Yeah, it sounds like a lot of work just to live there. Especially with all the rules that don't work. Also sounds like a lot of dying. I'm not about that life."

"It's not all that bad," Cece said. "You might love it, actually. You like solving problems, and it has a lot of problems to solve."

"Oh yeah? Like what?"

"Like, right now on the quest, WereDragon and I— WereDragon is this cool girl I met in Anarchia, and who I'm now questing with. Her real name is Aminata, though, right? So, she and I are trying to build the Wither I talked about last time."

Jo's eyes widened. "Wait . . . like you have to *build* the Wither, and *then* kill it?"

"I know, right? Insane."

"Wow. Your admin—the Ocury you called them? They're brutal."

"Yeah, they are. That's why I'm questing with Aminata. She's trying to become the next Ocury and make everything better. She's helping me complete the Second Trial, so that we can complete the Third Trial together. Then she'll get the XP she needs to become the next Ocury, and I'll get to Haven and find Therese. Win-win."

"Sounds nice," said Joachim.

"See?" Cece said. "You'd like it, really. Right now, we're trying to go get some soul sand to build the Wither with. It sounds like it won't be easy, but it still sounds like fun." She paused. "You know, you can come with if you like. One more hand in our quest wouldn't be bad. If you join, we can call ourselves an actual *crew*, like we're some badasses or something."

"Yeah," he said slowly. "But will your friend allow?"

"Who, Aminata?" Cece asked. "I don't think she'd have a problem with it. She'll probably even be happy for the extra hand.

Maybe when I get home, I'll add you on my console and send you a private message with the server address. Join whenever you want. Feel it out for yourself and then decide."

"Right," Joachim said, pensive. "Er, about that—I don't have a console, though."

"Oh?"

"Yeah. Granny is always saying we can't afford it. Not after paying school fees and whatnot. So I only just play games on my phone, including Minecraft."

"Oh. Okay. Maybe I'll just text you the server address, then."

Cece munched on her sandwich, embarrassed over having put Jo in this situation. She didn't want him to think she was like the estate kids, making a big deal simply because he didn't have a game unit. She didn't want him to feel awkward and have to explain himself about anything. Cece had experienced feeling different for liking Minecraft, and didn't want him to have that feeling about her. Especially because they both liked Minecraft, and it was the other little differences between them that made them such good friends anyway.

Break time ended, and they were headed back to class when they were stopped by Mr. Gbenga. Walking with him was Ofure, head down, looking compliant.

"Aha, I'm glad I caught you two on your way in," he said, motioning toward Ofure. "It seems your classmate has something to say to you."

Ofure lifted her head. Her face was tight in a way that said she had nothing for us but bitter anger.

"Ofure?" Mr. Gbenga goaded.

"Sorry," she said.

"For?" Mr. Gbenga insisted.

"For the things I said. And did."

"Which were?"

"Mean things," she muttered.

"Louder."

"Mean things."

"Good." Mr. Gbenga smiled at Joachim and Cece. "That'll do. Now, you two can be off to class. Ofure, you still have some work left on that punishment, yes? A thousand words saying *I will not be a bully* . . ."

He led Ofure away, and Cece and Joachim giggled to one another before heading back to class.

CHAPTER TWENTY

LATER THAT NIGHT, BEFORE SHE went to bed, Cece checked that Aminata had sent an invite to add her as a friend on the console's network. She had. Cece accepted the invite and then sent her a message:

Hi, it read. It's Cece. Just checking when you want to go to Anarchia next.

After that, she picked up her tablet and copied the server address Therese had sent her, then forwarded it to Joachim. She also copied the messages Therese had sent explaining all she needed to know. She edited them for Joachim's needs, then sent it all, along with one final note:

Once I get the location of the Soul Sand Valley, I'll text the coordinates to you, too. Then you can teleport and we'll meet you there.

Once it was sent, she saw there was a response from Aminata.

How about this weekend? she asked. *And every weekend after that? We can spend a ton of real hours playing so we can spend many days in the game and get to Haven quickly.*

It suddenly dawned on Cece that the journey might be over if they got to Haven so quickly. Did she want it to end? She wanted this to last for as long as possible—this feeling, this enjoyment. Especially as Joachim was probably going to join in soon, and they could all be a merry band, traversing Anarchia and saving everything that needed saving.

I have a friend, Cece wrote back. *Who wants to join the quest.*

There was a delay before Aminata wrote back: *Can they fight?*

Cece wrote back: *I don't know.*

I'm not sure I can protect two people, Aminata said.

He's good in many other things, Cece said. *He's the one who taught me how to complete the First Trial. All just by looking at the map.*

Sounds smart, Aminata said. *No problem. Bring him by.*

Do you have the location of the Soul Sand Valley?

Sure, Aminata wrote, and then provided the coordinates.

Cece copied them and forwarded them over to Joachim, then wrote to him: *Good luck!*

With that, she shut down her console and retired for the night with a smile on her lips.

The Soul Sand Valley is indeed, as Aminata described it, from the pit of hell.

We arrive at the location late, after leaving our hideout and crossing a huge chunk of desert for most of the sunset hours. We move with our eyes open and ears peeled, but there are so few mobs out here in the wastelands at this time that we easily dispatch the few we come across.

The entrance to the Soul Sand Valley is just a portal in the middle of the desert, surrounded by nothing but cacti. There's a gateway with a black frame and a purple sheen over the entrance. Sparkles fall like flakes from the sheen and drift into the air. Cranky leaps and tries to catch a few, but they disappear before reaching him.

"Okay," I say. "This is just creepy." I've come across talk of Nether realms and Soul Sand Valleys before on the internet, but I'd never bothered to look them up. This portal doesn't promise good vibes.

"Wait until you get inside," replies Aminata. She's about to enter when I say:

"Are we gonna wait for Jo or . . . ?"

Aminata looks around. "I don't see him here, do you?"

"Well no, but, like, I promised we'd meet him here. If we leave, how will he find us?"

"Maybe he'll be here before we're done getting our sand," she says. "Or else you'll just have to send him a new location or something when he's ready." Then she disappears through the door. I sigh and follow a moment later.

The world around me flips. I black out for a second, then come back to a loud, piercing sound, like a large beast's raspy breath. But I see no beast. All around me is darkness, so dark that even the sunset in the desert suddenly feels like light. The ground itself is some dark-colored sand. I can barely even see my own hands.

Aminata produces a torch and places it on the ground, and I look up.

The Soul Sand Valley is really a cavern. A massive, never-ending, dark cavern filled with all kinds of monstrous things. Lava, for starters. Lots and lots of lava everywhere, flowing down in different directions from the cavern's ceiling. The ceiling itself is undulating, like it has upside-down hills and mountains. I now see that the ground is made of the same kind of brown-and-gray material as everywhere else. But this material is special, in a way. It feels like it's moving, like it has its own life. This must be the prized soul sand.

The raspy-breathing sound has quieted down, but the hairs on my arms are still raised in anticipation.

"Do. Not. Move," Aminata says. "Just . . . freeze."

I do as told, and take the moment to look around. I see a bunch of Endermen spawning a few yards from us. But it's not just Endermen that populate this place.

I've never seen a ghast up close. I saw them once in a video, and simply thought they looked like a ghost because they were white and they floated. But now, I notice how eerie they seem, with just a large head and face attached to jellyfish-like tendrils. There's just one, not too far from us. It floats back and forth, but doesn't worry us.

There are other mobs, too. Another one with tendrils, just as huge but red and gray and with legs, walks over some lava. In another corner, I see what look like pigs, but with horns and ridges on their backs. They're in a herd of four, chittering and burbling as they pace about.

"Striders," Aminata says, watching me watch the mobs.

"Sorry?"

"The one moving on the lava is a strider. Completely harmless—I hear you can ride them like horses, if you want. But those other two . . ." She gestures at the ghast. "We get too close, and that ghast will shoot fireballs at us and explode on our heads. Huge damage." She gestures toward the herd in the corner? "Hoglins won't really attack unless we're closer than about thirty paces. Try to keep that distance from them both at all times."

"Wow," I say. "I can't wait to get out of here."

"So, dig," Aminata says, and begins mining the sand below her with a shovel. "You can use your hand. Don't go too far down—you never know what's down there. Just dig sideways, but stay in that spot. We don't want to take even a step farther in the direction of those hoglins or they'll run over here. Just pick up the few blocks around you, and let's get out. We only need four anyway."

I do as I'm told, and soon, we have an ample amount of soul sand in each of our inventories.

"All right," she says. "Back the way we came, in the exact same straight line."

I do as she says, and soon, we cross the portal again. The world tumbles, and the darkness gives way to the light of sunset in Anarchia. It suddenly feels like the brightest thing I've ever seen.

"Wow." I shiver. "That's the creepiest place we've been so far."

"They don't call it the Nether for nothing," Aminata says. "This one is just a small mod with one cavern. Imagine if we had a whole Nether in Anarchia. We'd be doomed." She looks around. "Your friend still isn't here."

I look around, too. It's nearing night, and Joachim is still nowhere to be found.

"You told him we'd be here, right?" she asks.

"Yes," I say. "Can we make tonight's hideout nearby? Maybe he'll be here once night is over."

"Okay," Aminata says. "But if he isn't here tomorrow, we may have to leave. We don't want to risk getting killed by Anarchians and losing all the soul sand and Wither skulls we've collected."

"Okay," I say, but think, *Please, Joachim. Where are you?*

———

The next morning, we come out of our hideout, not too far away from the Soul Sand Valley portal. Joachim is still nowhere in sight.

"Maybe you should tell him to meet us in the mountains," Aminata says.

"The mountains? Won't it be harder for him to find us there?"

"Maybe. But we can't stay here, waiting. We'll be easy pickings. We need to always be moving."

I look around again. *Come on, come on, Jo!* Had he changed his mind? Had I done something to cause this delay? Did I spoil our friendship somehow? The same way I'd almost ruined my friendship with Therese by destroying Silver Oaks?

Is this what I'm good at — ruining my friendships? I look across at Aminata, who looks impatient now, pacing and looking around for any nearby threats. *If I ask her to wait some more, would I make her angry and ruin this friendship, too?*

Friendships have up-and-down moments, I hear Iya's voice in my head say. *But that's okay.*

"Okay," I say. "The mountains it is."

CHAPTER TWENTY-ONE

THE JOURNEY TO THE MOUNTAINS takes up a whole day. Aminata makes us move without stopping, but eating and eating to ensure our strength does not go down. We slice through the few mobs we come across. We pass by a mob spawner once, and that is the only time we have to engage with more mobs than expected. We still come out on top.

We also come across a few Anarchians, mostly alone or in pairs like us. No large crews like Declan's. Aminata wants us to attack them, just to be sure they don't get the chance to attack us first. It's an opportunity for her to gather some more XP, too, just in case. But I feel bad about it, and tell her so. She huffs, but decides each time to respect my wishes.

Just before sunset is over, we arrive at the mountain range.

On my map of Anarchia, the mountains looked like just squiggly lines. But now that we're here next to them, they are massive, towering stacks of sand and stone and grass, capped with snow at their tips. Every hill and dip has an extreme slope with many cliffs, a few of them sporting waterfalls. They rise so high into the skies that I know it will be impossible to climb over them without risking falling to instant death.

"Whoa," I say, looking so far up that I almost fall backward.

"Yeah," says Aminata. "Massive, isn't it?"

"Totally." I check my map quickly to be sure that this is the right range. It seems to be.

"Do you know if anyone has ever tried to climb over it?" I ask Aminata. "Like, to get to the other side without maybe completing the Second Trial?"

"Oh, I've tried that, hee-hee," she says. "It just kicks you back down once you get to the peak. You don't even get to see over to the other side. And even then, I hear there's nothing on the other side, just . . . blankness."

"Hmm," I say. "So how does the beacon do the thing where it takes us to the other side?"

"I think it acts like some kind of portal," she says. "You know, just like the Soul Sand Valley. The beacon kinda opens up a portal that takes us to the dimension where we complete the Third Trial. But I still don't know what that dimension is. I could never see it before getting mobbed. We do this right, and we'll know soon enough."

She starts climbing, and I follow her. We divide the labor of climbing, she picking up blocks and placing them below her for me to step on, me doing the same for Cranky below.

Soon, we get to a high enough spot, almost into the snow. She pauses and looks around, unsure.

"What is it?" I ask.

"Shoot," she says. "I don't think I can find the cave I used last time."

"Can't we find a new one?"

"Well, yeah. But then we'll have to dig it specially to fight the Wither. And digging in new mountain caves is unpredictable."

"Why?"

"Well, for one thing, we will def meet some hostile mobs, because it's always dark in there. Fighting them is always tricky, because we can easily fall. Also, there can be abandoned mines in there that we can fall through unknowingly. Then there's the silverfish."

"Silverfish?"

"Yeah. They're small but deadly hostile mobs. They hide inside the stone here and can just pop out and attack you while you're digging."

"Wow."

"Yeah." She looks around. "It's getting darker, though, so let's just dig a small hideout here and chill for the night. We'll figure something out before next sunset."

We do figure something out before next sunset. It's to dig a new cave where we'll build and fight the Wither.

"So, what do we do about Joachim?" I ask, as Aminata surveys the mountains for the best spot to start digging.

"We can get to him after we beat the Wither," she says. "Let's just focus on getting this done for now."

"And what if we don't beat it?" I ask.

She shoots me a sharp look. "Why wouldn't we?"

"I dunno, because it's, like, strong? I hear it has like fifteen times our health points."

"Yup, it does."

"So . . ."

"So we hit it fifteen times more than it can hit us."

"Ugh." I pace around. "I think having Joachim here would've helped us beat it easier."

"True," she says. "But he's not here and we can't wish him into existence. So let's just do what we can."

We begin digging. First, a tunnel: one block wide, two blocks high. Aminata lays out the plan.

"So, first thing is, the Wither needs to be trapped when we fight it," she says as we dig. "Otherwise it can fly away and dodge our attacks. So, at the end of this tunnel, we'll build a room just small enough to contain the Wither. Once you spawn it, we run back down this tunnel. Fast."

"Why?"

"Because it'll start growing, and then explode." She places a torch. "Causing a massive explosion that'll take out many blocks. And we can't attack it before then because it'll be invulnerable. But once it has exploded, we'll start shooting it with arrows. It'll be trapped here and unable to escape them. Your arrows plus mine, then we move in with our swords."

"Sounds simple." I place another torch. We've gone through dirt and moved into stone now. "Why is it so simple?"

"Oh, it's not. In between all that shooting, the Wither won't just be looking at us. As we hit it, it'll break any block around it. Which means it'll be breaking this tunnel, and we'll have to keep moving back. It has a dash attack and can also shoot Wither skulls at us. If they hit us, we get something called the 'Wither effect.' A kind of poison that drains your health."

"Wow," I say, placing another torch.

"Don't worry," she says. "I have some buckets of milk to cure that. We'll share."

We keep digging and placing torches. So far, we haven't come upon any mobs or infested blocks that contain silverfish. But we're a long way away from the entrance. Cranky, who has followed us inside, *rawrs* to inform me of his discomfort with the situation.

"You and me both, dude," I say.

"Okay, this is enough," Aminata says at some point. "Let's eat, and then do the room."

We do the room really quick, making a small opening with a torch or two, placed in a way that the Wither's blast won't completely destroy them.

Then, it's time to build our monster.

"You have to be the one to spawn it," Aminata says. "That's the only way it records you completing the Second Trial."

I place the blocks as instructed. First, one block of soul sand with three above it to form a T shape. Then, each of the three Wither skulls upon the top three soul sand blocks. Aminata tells me that as soon as I place the last one, the Wither will spawn.

When I'm done, with only the last skull in my hand, ready to drop, I ask Aminata, "Ready?"

"Wait," she says. "I need to give you a few things to prepare you for the fight."

She starts to drop some items. I pick them all up:

- 3 buckets of milk
- 4 pieces of bread
- 1 golden apple
- 2 Strength potions
- 18 arrows

"The milk is for the Wither effect," she says. "If a skull hits you, drink it immediately. The bread is for quenching your hunger quickly; all that fighting takes energy. The golden apple is your last resort, for when anything goes wrong. You get hunger points, but also some extra health and regeneration for a short while. Only use the golden apple if all hell breaks loose."

"Okay. What are these Strength potions for?"

"Drink one when you switch to a sword. Increases your attack damage. About halfway through the fight, drink another one. Helps finish the Wither off quicker."

"Cool! Why so many arrows, though?"

"I've given you eighteen because that's how many you'll need before the Wither starts becoming immune to them. After that, we'll have to go in with swords. You'll have to damage it at least twenty-five times—about half its full health—for this to record as your Second Trial. I told you, the Ocury is sly—they don't tell anyone this. I found out the hard way. So don't shoot your arrows if you're going to miss. Draw, wait until you have the opening, then fire."

I repeat everything she has told me under my breath, arranging and rearranging the items in my hotbar for easy pick and use.

"Still have the Potion of Regeneration and iron sword I gave you in your forest base?"

"Yeah?"

"Add those to your hotbar, too. It's going to suck once arrows stop working and you have to change to a sword. As a rule, just don't go too close unless you have to. If you've somehow used everything else up, pull out your sword, use any Regeneration and Strength potions left, and charge in."

"Wouldn't that be, like, suicide?"

"Probably. But what a good way to go, right?"

I look at all the items in my hotbar and say a silent prayer.

"Remember," Aminata says. "Place skull and what?"

"Run. Far down the tunnel. Wait for explosion. Then start shooting."

"All right, quester. Time to claim your prize."

I breathe and walk forward, the last Wither skull in my hand. I hold it up, out, and am about to place it when . . .

"Cece!" The inbuilt narration reads me a message from an unidentified player. "Cece!"

I whip around. Someone is running down the tunnel, toward Aminata and me. They're wearing iron armor and holding an iron sword, but other than that have nothing else that helps me recognize them.

Until I look at the player name tag and see they have opted to reveal it: JoJo_Hobbit.

"Jo?" I say. "Is that you?"

"They're coming!" he's saying. "All of them—they're coming!"

"Stay back!" Aminata pulls out a diamond sword. "I said stay—"

"Who's coming?" I ask. "Wait—how did you find—"

"I went to the location you gave me," he's saying, running forward. "They were there—an ambush. Like they knew I was coming. Well, that *you* were coming. I ran—they pursued me—"

"Where are they?" Aminata cuts in. "Did they follow you—"

"I saw you two from a distance—"

"I said 'Did they follow you'!?" Aminata is screaming now.

"I don't know, but yes they were behind me in the beginning—"

"Oh, shoot!" Aminata says, looking at me, but also looking past me, into the room behind me.

I turn around as a rumble begins to shake the very foundations of the small room we've built at the end of the tunnel. It takes me a moment to realize that the skull I was holding in my hand is gone. Between all the quarreling and shouting, I must've mistakenly placed it. And now, instead of the soul sand and skulls that had been there a second before, a freshly spawned three-headed black-and-gray monster towers above me.

The Wither lets out a chilling, deathly growl.

"What in the—" says Joachim.

"Run!" screams Aminata, and all of us, Cranky included, turn and scamper down the tunnel as quickly as our legs can carry us.

All I can hear is the increasingly loud growls of the Wither as it begins to grow, sending the hairs on the back of my neck rising and a tremor racing through my bones. I try to stay focused, try to remember everything Aminata has taught me so far. *Strength, arrows, bread, milk, Regeneration.* I recite them in my head to calm myself, counting down slowly to when the Wither explodes and we can start attacking it.

Which is why I don't see the other end of the tunnel, the one we're now facing, darken with the appearance of a band of Anarchians.

Aminata sees them first, and she screeches to a halt. Joachim bumps into her, and I into Joachim.

"Hello, WereDragon," says Declan, stepping into the tunnel and blocking it off. "And WereDragon's friend. Well, *friends.*"

Two of his crew members, all diamond armor, break a few blocks and step in after him, so that all three of them have blocked the tunnel proper. We're well and truly trapped.

The Wither's growls reverberate through the tunnel. Declan and his crew stop short.

"Is that . . . ?" Declan asks. "Nooo, you can't be serious. Did you really?" He laughs, *heeheehee.* "Well, well, it seems one of us is going to get you today, WereDragon." He pulls out his sword. "Time to choose which hand you will perish by."

Aminata pulls out her own sword and swings it at the ready. "Not by yours, if I can help it."

"Charge!" Declan says, and leads his crew into a run toward us.

Then the Wither explodes and all hell breaks loose.

CHAPTER TWENTY-TWO

I'VE NEVER BEEN IN A fight before, IRL or even in here, in Anarchia. Not to mention a melee in a narrow corridor, bodies colliding with one another, and a three-headed monster five times my size bearing down on me.

I freeze.

I'm not sure how long I stand there, lost in time, all sound faded from my ears, watching blocks shatter around me as players and Wither alike yell and shriek and roar.

Then I'm jerked back into the present by someone shouting my name.

"Cece!" It's Aminata, who's warding off Declan and another crew member, while Joachim keeps busy the remaining crew members who've entered the tunnel. Jo dances about, dodging their swipes.

"Cece!" Aminata is saying, looking over her shoulder at me in the split second before she repels another Declan attack. "Kill it!"

"They can't harm you because of Cranky!" Joachim adds. "Face the Wither!"

So I turn around, my back to the fight with Declan's crew, and face the monster.

Thanks to our shouts of *"Run!"* we're still a long distance away from the Wither in the room at the end of the tunnel. But no thanks to the explosion, the Wither has created more room for itself and is crunching its way toward us, toward me. Every block it touches shatters into pieces, earning it a step forward. Worse, it has started to shatter even more surrounding blocks, including a few black ones: infested blocks. They shatter, and two gray insect-like creatures creep out, hiss, and begin advancing toward me.

"Shikes," I mutter, drawing out my iron sword. "Silverfish." I take out the first Strength potion and drink like my life depends on it.

The silverfish, black eyes and porcupine-like bodies and all, move fast in their skittering footsteps. But they also die surprisingly fast—just one swish of my sword, and they're gone with one last hiss. I quickly switch over to my bow, nock an arrow, train it on the Wither, and fire.

It hits the target.

One down, I tell myself. Fifty-eleven to go.

Behind me, the sounds of fighting intensify. I can hear them all screaming, the voice-to-text-to-speech translations of their grunts and groans all wrong and muddled up, so that they sound like a chorus of chaos. But I refuse to turn around and look, putting all my faith in my grumpy stray cat, knowing he will glitch and swallow or whatever to protect me. I place all my focus on what's at the end of the tunnel. True tunnel vision, if ever.

I back up and release another strengthened arrow. It hits. Back up again, shoot another. Another hit. The Wither screeches in anger and breaks more blocks, inching ever so slightly toward me. I backtrack and release again. Another, another. Six hits so far.

Then the Wither locks eyes with me, shudders, and shoots three Wither skulls.

Crap! "Duck!" I scream, then crouch and shift my weight.

The first skull flies past me, as does the second. Behind me, there's an *oof*, the sound of a player taking a hit, going *poof!* From the voice, I know it's not Jo or Aminata. One of Declan's, though I do not look.

Because the third skull, which is a tad slower than the first two, smacks me square in the chest.

My whole body shudders, and my health takes a swift dip. But it doesn't just stop there. It starts to deteriorate even further, the Wither effect taking hold.

"*Milk, milk, milk,*" I mutter to myself, frantically searching my hotbar for the bucket. I find it just as I'm down to two hearts of health, and drink it quickly. Then I pluck the Potion of Regeneration and do the same. My health begins to tick back up. I chomp on two pieces of bread to quench my hunger.

"Well, now I'm pissed." I pull out my bow and let off four sharp shots in rapid succession. Two miss, two hit the Wither. It growls, trying to find me in the tunnel, breaking more blocks. I shoot another three arrows. All three hit the Wither. But because neither of them is fully drawn, the damage is minimal. It feels like throwing darts at an elephant.

So I just start shooting sporadically. Hit, miss, hit, miss, it doesn't matter. Anything to get this monster off my back, to prevent it from breaking those blocks and getting to me. Especially now that I've retreated to my last possible point, my back now touching Joachim's as he repels more and more of Declan's crew.

The next arrow I shoot bounces off the Wither without doing any damage. I shoot another. Same thing. That's when I notice the Wither has gone past half-health. There is a sound, like a charge, and a glowing shield surrounds it. Then it summons three Wither skeletons.

Crap!

Luckily, Jo is suddenly there.

I have to go closer.

So I do as Aminata advised: I drink the last Strength potion, pull out my sword, and go charging in.

I've not even gotten two strikes at the Wither when it swipes at me and sends me hurtling back down the corridor I came from. My health swings down to less than two-fifths of itself. I pull out the golden apple, chomp on it, and fly back at the Wither. I slash, slash, slash, hitting it just enough times to matter. But for each of my many slashes, it manages to get me at least once or twice. Thanks to the golden apple, though, my regeneration happens quickly, and I still get in a few more hits before I can make my way back into the tunnel for a brief reprieve.

By this time, the Wither has exploded its room so much that it now has enough space to move. And it does just that, settles down, and shoots another three skulls in my direction.

I dodge the first. I do not dodge the second, nor the third.

After the first skull hits me, I pull out a bucket of milk. The second one hits me just as I'm chugging the milk. As a result I don't get the Wither effect, but my health goes down to critical: only half a heart left!

Oh no, I think. *It's over.*

I still need to get in at least five more hits before I can completely take out the Wither. My golden apple is gone, Strength and Regeneration potions gone, arrows useless. There's no way I'm going to get those five hits in with just half a heart. I'll get hit, and it'll be good night for me.

Then, I have an idea.

It's been so long since the battle with the evoker that I completely forgot I had it: the Totem of Undying. Just the exact thing I need in this place. If I'm holding it in at least one hand when I get final fatal damage, it saves me.

So I pull it out of my inventory and slot it into my off-hand—my left. With my main hand—my right—I grab my sword.

"How do you like my dual wield, monster?" I say. Then I charge into the room.

I will never accurately remember what happens next. All I know is that I'm in there, slashing and slashing, getting good chunks out of the Wither but also missing it a good bit. I think I get maybe four hits when it shoots a fresh three skulls at me.

All three skulls strike me in the chest.

For a half-second, there is a blackout. I'm definitely sure this is the end for me. My second-to-last life in Anarchia gone, lost. *Only one life left to complete two Trials*, I think. *I'll never get to Haven.*

Then there is a loud sound, like glass breaking, or a large diamond shattering.

But it is not a large diamond shattering. It is the Totem of Undying.

A surge powers through my body, like I am being awoken from the dead. My health is rejuvenated and starts to refill rapidly, the regeneration effect of the totem kicking in. But even better, its

Absorption effect joins in, giving me four more hearts of health. I feel like a superhero, a machine, a god.

And I know there will be no better time to finish the Wither off than this.

"I will get to Haven," I say, drawing my sword, a growl of confidence creeping into my voice. "And you can't stop me."

I charge at the Wither.

It's almost like it smells my eagerness, like it knows it will be taking its last breath, too. So it shrieks, shudders, rears its heads— all three of them—and spits its last three skulls at me.

The first strikes me in the chest, but I don't stop charging. The second strikes me, and my health takes a dive. Still, I stride forward. The third hits me and my health dips, nearing its end, but none of that is enough to stop me. *I will get to Haven. I will see my friend.*

I lift my sword and strike the Wither with my last blow.

The monster quakes, convulses as if possessed by jitters. Then it lets out an eerie scream, one that seems to go on forever and ever and ever.

Then suddenly, it's all over. **Second Trial Completed!** my chatbox announces, as green XP drops over my head. *Congratulations!*

Where the monster once was now sits a lone Nether star. I trudge toward it on my last legs, my health still deteriorating, and pick it up.

Nether star! says my chatbox.

But my health is still deteriorating, going critical, with no indication of stopping. I suddenly realize: I never cured the Wither effect from the last three skulls!

I pull out my last bucket of milk just as my health is almost at zero. The edges of my vision are now darkening, going closer and closer to nothingness. I can see the tunnel, can make out bodies, still fighting—or not? I can't tell who is who, and can't even tell if it's a person or the cat. I can't tell whether the player who seems to be turning toward me is Joachim or Aminata or Declan. I can hear them calling my name, though. *Cece! Cece! Cece . . .*

I drink the milk as quickly as I can. For a moment, nothing happens. And then—

CHAPTER TWENTY-THREE

"CECE!" BABA STEPPED INTO THE den and removed the headphones from Cece's head, then slipped the controller out of her hands. "Hey!" He snapped his fingers in her ears.

Cece jumped back into the real world, blinking like a zombie.

"What do you think you're doing?" Baba was saying. "Are you seeing the time? It might be Friday, but you can't be up at this time playing games!"

Cece blinked at the clock. It was half past one. In the morning.

"I might have just died," she said, slowly.

Baba was taken aback. "Excuse me?"

"I might've just died," Cece repeated, "when you pulled me out of the game like that. That was the toughest fight of my life, and I might've just won it, but you might've just killed me, too."

Baba held a hand to his chest. "Wow, okay, don't scare me like that! I thought you were talking about real life." Then a small frown appeared on his forehead. "I'm not sure I like how you get so immersed in this game each time you play. Especially with all this talk of fights and killing. What's really going on here, Cece? It's almost two in the morning and you're not even in your pajamas yet!"

Cece looked at herself, only now realizing she was still in her school blouse. She could remember so little about the day's events. The whole school week seemed like a blur, like it had ended a long time ago and not just a few hours earlier. The only part she remembered was seeing Joachim at closing time and telling him to be sure to join Aminata and her at the location she had given him. Anarchia was starting to become more real to her than the world out here.

"I was trying to complete something so I can find Therese," said Cece.

"Huh?" Baba scratched his head. "That makes no sense."

"It's . . . complicated."

"I'm sure it is," Baba said. "But I'm not going to stand here and hear it. All gaming tonight is done. I'm going to shut it all down, and now you must go to bed."

"Wait!" Cece said, as Baba moved to pull the plug. "Can I at least Save and Quit first?"

Baba paused, looked at his daughter, confused but understanding. He nodded. "Fair enough."

So Cece quickly pressed the Save button, gave it a half-minute to be sure, then shut down the system. She didn't know for sure what had just happened in there. Yes, she had completed the Second Trial, but was she now down to her last life? Did she still have the Nether star? What had happened to Joachim and Aminata, both fighting Declan's crew?

These questions she would have to get answers to later, as she turned off the lights and exited the den under Baba's watchful stare. He followed her until she had changed into her pajamas and brushed her teeth, then tucked her into bed.

"Good night, kiddo," he said, and paused. "Sorry if I was a bit harsh on you earlier. I understand you miss your friend. But you understand this is not the only way to contact her, right? I could ask around the estate or something. Someone somewhere must have access to Mr. Njinga's new number. I could find you a way to speak to your friend. But I don't want you staying up late just for that."

"It's not just for—" Cece sighed. "It's not just about Therese. Yes, when I started, I just really wanted to find her. But now, I also have other friends on there, and they need my help."

"Well, that's nothing that can't wait until tomorrow, is it? In fact, it can wait until next week. We planned to go to the estate Independence Day party, remember? Maybe you should take this weekend off games completely. Spend some time out there in the open. Maybe make some new friends out here in the real world."

"They *are* my real-world friends," Cece rebutted.

"Okay, okay, fine," Baba acceded. "Let's make a deal then. Stay off gaming this weekend—not even on the tablet!—and I'll see what I can do to get you back in contact with Therese. Deal?"

Cece sighed. "Fine. Deal."

"Good," he said. "Sleep tight." He turned off the light and shut the door, plunging the room into near darkness.

Cece shut her eyes and breathed a sigh of relief. She was indeed drowsy, now that she was no longer feeding on the game's adrenaline. Maybe she could watch a few videos to fall asleep.

She pulled out the tablet, which she sometimes hid under the bedclothes for this very reason. But just as she was about to open the video streaming app, she spotted the notification bar.

Messages. From Joachim.

The first was a frantic *Where are you?* Then two periods, as if he'd been typing too fast and mistyped. The last message was written just as frantically, but as Cece read it, everything about her seemed to slow down.

Aminata, it read. *She's gone.*

The weekend dragged on like a snail. Sleep came to Cece in fits and starts, and she woke up much too early and spent the day all crabby. Her hands itched all day to reach for her console, just to check that Aminata was still there, that *she* herself was still there, alive. But she kept to the deal with Baba and stayed away. Not that she could have played even if she'd tried, though. Baba had ensured she'd stay true to their deal by removing the power adapter, ensuring she couldn't switch her console on.

Meanwhile, Gemshore Estate was having the time of its life. On October 1 each year, the estate spared no expense in celebrating Nigeria's Independence Day. So, this weekend, just like every other independence weekend, residents strung green-and-white lights everywhere they could and draped green-and-white silk from their windows. They tucked little Nigerian flags between their wipers and on their dashboards. At least one house down the same street as the Alao house hoisted a real-life flag, flapping tall and proud in the evening breeze.

The celebrations culminated in the estate's independence dance party on Sunday. The party was often held in the small green park in the center of the estate. It was a sizeable field that could contain every family in the estate plus friends. Iya had suggested Cece invite Joachim, and she had texted him to ask if he wanted to come by. He'd taken an awfully long time to respond, but when he eventually did, he said he'd try to show up.

So, it ended up that on Sunday evening, Cece stood alone in a corner of the party, attending for the first time without Therese. Watching the party unfold brought back memories of all their fun moments here together, including everything from tasting every dish to joining in the games. But today, Cece didn't feel like doing anything. Besides, she didn't want to ruin her dress.

She was dressed in the same green-black-and-white Ankara fabric as everyone else, shared weeks before between every household, for each to make their own clothes out of. Her dress was elegant, flared and with cutoff arms. She loved it to bits, and it was the only reason she was here, just to show it off. That, and because Iya allowed her to have her hair plaited at a hairdresser's and not at home. And also because of the deal with Baba, of course.

Music boomed from the speakers, and there was food and drink everywhere. Fried rice, chicken, small chops, even pounded yam and Egusi soup and other dishes. But Cece was not enjoying herself. She held a cup of her favorite hibiscus juice in her hand and stood in a corner, watching everyone else dance to Afrobeats music.

Someone tapped her shoulder. She turned around, and it was Joachim. He was all dressed up in a way she had never seen him before. All-white sneakers, a T-shirt with a fancy clockwork owl, a new haircut. Cece liked him for that—that he looked good and felt good enough to come back here. Take that, mean estate kids.

"Happy Independence Day!" he said, and high-fived her.

"You, too," she said, then pulled a nearby chair over for him to sit on before she pulled over another for herself and did the same.

Just then, Iya wandered over and spotted Joachim.

"Jo, you came!" She embraced him in a welcome, then asked: "Have you eaten? Lemme get you some food." She yelled at someone passing by with a tray of food, and they handed down a plate of chicken and rice to Joachim and asked what he wanted to drink. He asked for a Coke.

"So," Joachim said over the booming music as he ate, "I haven't seen you in Anarchia."

"I've been banned," Cece said. "For the weekend, at least. My dad and I have a kind of deal going."

"Oh, okay. When are you coming back? It's boring there without you both."

"Monday," she said, then turned to face him. "And about that. Tell me: What exactly happened to Aminata?"

He put up a hand to signal to her that he wanted to finish his food before he started his story. Cece waited impatiently until he had eaten his chicken down to the bone, chugged his Coke, and let out a huge burp.

"Eew," she said. "Manners, dude."

He laughed. "Sorry. I forget myself sometimes." He cleared his throat. "So. Aminata."

"Is she . . . dead?"

He waited a moment, then nodded slowly.

"Did you see it happen?"

He delayed again before nodding.

"Tell me how it happened."

He just shrugged. "Declan. We fought and fought, but there were just too many of them. Even I was only able to survive be-

cause some of those skulls you dodged hit the guys I was fighting."
He puffed up his cheeks. "It's all my fault. If I hadn't led them to
you people—"

"Don't say that," Cece said. "It's not your fault. You didn't
know there was an ambush."

"Can you apologize to her for me? I know she's been stacking
up XP, and I know you lose a small chunk of them each time you
die. I'll go with her to get them back if I have to."

"I can only contact her through my console, so that'll be Monday, I guess," Cece said. "You've been to Anarchia since then.
Have you seen her yet? Do you know if she's still alive?"

Joachim shrugged again.

"I really hope she's okay. I wanted us to do it together, you
know? Complete the Trials, get to Haven, defeat the Ocury, see
Therese again." Cece sighed. "I hope we still can."

Party music boomed and filled the estate park. Cece and
Joachim walked the periphery, stopping to watch some of the
party attractions. There was a guy doing card tricks, including
making cards disappear and retrieving them from inside people's
food. It was hilarious. Cece and Joachim laughed and laughed at
how dumbfounded the people looked.

Cece realized she was more comfortable being herself when
Joachim was around, and that he was the closest thing to a best
friend she'd had since Therese. She thought it would be great to
have him over every weekend like she had Therese. Especially
now that Therese was in another time zone. So long as they
avoided the snotty estate kids, of course. They had avoided them
so far at the party, and all was well.

"You know how to dance?" Joachim asked, moving toward the
middle of the field, where everyone who cared to was dancing.

"Nope," Cece confessed. "My friend Reesa—she used to say I don't have a dancing bone in my body."

"Then we're the same," he said, laughing. "I can't dance to save my life."

"Then why are you going there?"

"Because who cares?" he said. "Dancing is fun anyway, so I'm gonna do it."

He shuffled toward the center, wiggling his bottom and shifting his body this way and that. Cece laughed and laughed and called him an old man. Then, after a while, she went and joined him.

CHAPTER TWENTY-FOUR

ONCE THE WEEKEND AND THE party were over, Baba came back to Cece with updates about his search for Mr. Njinga's phone number.

"I've touched base with a few people," he said. "Good news: Mrs. Olumide from three streets down does have his most recent number. Bad news: she's away on vacation and has turned off all communication for now. But I hear she'll be back next week, so we won't have to wait long."

But Cece wasn't quite as worried about contacting Therese as she was about finding out if Aminata was fine. Therese was in Haven—she was okay. Aminata was the one who really needed her help right now.

So, very early on Monday morning, before her parents woke up, Cece rose and returned to her now reinstated console. She put her headphones over her ears and turned it on.

Hi, she wrote to Aminata via the messaging window. **Jo told me what happened. I'm sorry. And Jo is, too.**

She paused, then added: I'll still help you complete the Third Trial and get your XP so you can become the Ocury. If you want.

Then she stopped her messaging and went to school.

For most of the day, there was little time for Cece to think of Anarchia or Aminata. October meant the school year had just begun to pick up steam, and more teachers were demanding more and more from students. Between trying to reconnect with Therese and surviving Anarchia, Cece had barely had time to start getting used to secondary school, and it was starting to hit her in the face.

Her grades had not begun to slip yet, but she was having trouble with some subjects. First period was math as usual. Mr. Gbenga had just introduced them to algebra, and Cece couldn't wrap her head around it. Then, in basic science the next period, she struggled with distinguishing between renewable and non-renewable energies. Luckily, Joachim agreed to help her catch up during break time, after she asked. They spent the time at their table in the food court poring over notes. It meant they didn't get any time to talk about Anarchia, though.

But after break time wasn't any better. The teacher for Hausa language was a woman who spoke too quickly for Cece to grasp what she was saying, whether she was speaking to them in English or Hausa. It didn't get better when she started teaching them Rubutun wasika, or letter writing.

At the end of the school day, Cece felt tired and beaten to her bones. On the ride home, Iya looked over at her, quiet in the front seat.

"Rough day, eh?" Iya asked.

"Like, the roughest," Cece said.

"*Eyaa, pẹlẹ,*" said Iya. "Sorry. It gets better, don't worry. At least now you have a friend going through the same thing with you. It's always better when you don't have to do it alone."

Cece thought about this the whole ride home, and once she had undressed, had some lunch, and it was leisure time, she checked in on her message to Aminata.

Still no response.

But, surprisingly, the player list panel showed that one player was online right now: WereDragon_86.

So, Cece slipped on her headphones, picked up her controller, and plunged back into the world of Anarchia.

Something isn't right.

Coming back into the world of Anarchia happens slowly, like my body is starting all over again. Maybe that's because it is.

I don't wake up in the mountain cave where we defeated the Wither and fought off Declan's crew. Instead, I find myself standing in a small, cramped room with nothing but a torch. It takes me awhile to remember it as the last hideout we'd dug and slept in, right before going out to attack the Wither.

I died, I realize with a growing dread.

My first instinct is to quickly look in my inventory. I almost jump with joy when I find that the Nether star is still there. One life lost, all right, but the prize remains.

I suddenly realize that the hideout isn't empty. Aminata is there, standing in a corner, unmoving, probably AFK at the moment. She's not in her diamond armor, but in plain clothes, which I've never quite seen her in before. She has shocking blue hair, and wears red-and-black clothes patterned to look like fire. On her feet are brown leather boots. I'm unsure if she's AFK or actually present, and I'm about to ask when she suddenly turns around.

"Whoa," I say. "Scared me there. Hey."

"Hey," she says.

"Saw you were online, so I came," I say. "I don't . . ." I drift off. "I don't know what to say. I just came here to be with you, if that's okay."

"Okay," Aminata says.

We stay like that for a while, saying nothing, but understanding each other all the same. There's a comfort in just being here, being sad together about our respective fates. She may never get to replace the Ocury and bring some kindness to this world.

"I saw your messages," Aminata finally says. "Thanks. They helped me not feel so bad."

"Yeah," I say. "I just didn't want you to be angry with me, or with Joachim." I paused. "Are you? Angry?"

"No," says Aminata. "I know he was only trying to help."

"Okay."

"But you two don't have to worry about helping me anymore, anyway. I've decided to quit."

"What?"

"Yeah," she says. "That's what I decided just now, as I was AFK. What's the point? I have just one life left, and you have just one, too—I saw you die after killing the Wither. If either one of us dies before we complete the Third Trial, it's all over. No Haven, no new Ocury, and we can never get back into Anarchia again. Forever."

This realization washes over me like a bucket of water. But I refuse to be fazed. So I stubbornly push away all the doubt trying to crush me, and instead say:

"No."

Aminata looks up. "No?"

"No," I repeat. "You will not give up. *We* are not giving up."

"We're not?"

"No, we're not." Confidence creeps into my voice. "We are going to complete that Third Trial. I am going to get into Haven, and you are going to become the next Ocury."

"And what if we die?"

"Then we die trying," I say. "It doesn't matter if we have one life or ten. What matters is that we tried. It's better than not trying at all, right?"

She's thoughtful for a moment, then says, "Yeah."

"So get up off your butt and stop moping. We have a Trial to complete."

But I still feel like something is missing. It takes me awhile before I realize what it is.

"Wait," I say. "Where's Cranky?"

"Right. About that," she says. "They must've taken him."

"They *what*!?" Anger burns inside me. "Oh, now Declan and I have a problem."

"We should go get him back," she says. "Together."

I look at her. "Really?"

"Really."

"Are you sure? Last time—"

"Forget about last time," she says. "If we're going to at least have fun while we do this, then we do everything we want. You, me, Jo. Together."

"Okay," I say, suddenly reinvigorated. "We go get Cranky. *Then* we complete that Third Trial and you can fix this cruel world once and for all."

CHAPTER TWENTY-FIVE

FIRST, WE TELL JOACHIM WHERE to find us. This I did after friending him. Then we waited for him to make his way over in-game. Now we're in the hideout, going over the map and trying to decipher how to find Declan.

"They have a base not too far from the village," says Aminata. "Anarchians call it the Iron Fortress, because they built many parts of it with large iron blocks and it's very difficult to get into. There's just too many of them, and with all the cheats from the Ocury that they have, it's literally impossible to defeat them."

"So we don't try to defeat them," I say. "We just sneak in when they're not around and steal Cranky back."

"I don't think they'll leave the Talisman of Chance behind," Joachim says. "Sounds like something you take with you everywhere so no one steals it."

"He's right," says Aminata. "We'll have to do it some other way."

"I know," says Joachim. "What if we slip into the fortress when they're not home, and hide? Then, when they return, we wait for them to log off, steal Cranky, and run."

"Ooh," I say, "that sounds . . . doable." Aminata thinks so, too, as she's nodding her head.

"Yes," she says. "We can, like, hide in the walls or whatever. Especially the non-iron walls. Declan is probably the one who carries Cranky, and he's such a control freak. He never logs off. Ever. We'll just see where he ties the cat's lead when he goes AFK. Then Cece, you'll feed him fish or something and he'll be back with you again. We can get out before they even wake up."

It sounds like a good plan, so we all get working on it.

First, we try to pinpoint the location on the in-game map I snagged from the boy in the village. I drop the map for Jo who, not as much a skilled fighter as Aminata, is more of a problem-solver. He manages to narrow it down to a general area just by guessing around and fiddling with numbers I don't bother to ask about. In his selected area, we pick a spot a bit farther out so that we know exactly how close or far we are and aren't surprised by anything. Then, we each look in our inventories. I'm mostly empty of big resources, and my iron sword is almost used up, but I have food and tools, at least. Better than having nothing.

Aminata and Jo seem to be in the same situation, but overall, we have what it takes to make the journey. So we set out immediately.

Crossing the desert again is less daunting than before. We fight off more mobs than last time, but we do it in half the time, because we do it without fear, and that gets us through. That, and the added advantage of Joachim's help with direction. When we finally arrive at the Iron Fortress, it is deserted, as expected. That doesn't mean it's not guarded, though. There is a pack of four wolves, each one guarding one of the four main entrances to the building.

From where we stand, surveying the structure, I can see why everyone calls it the Iron Fortress. It is indeed a fortress, built into the side of a stone hill, its front façade made of iron blocks. There are some oak trees for decoration, and some wheat, potato, and sugarcane growing along one side. There is a small farm with pigs and chickens. A couple of horses are leashed to a nearby post, evidence of Declan and his crew's possible friendship with the Ocury, as horses are very hard to come by in Anarchia. Overall, it's a real nice homestead, if only it weren't being run by a massive jerk.

"We'll never get in if the owners of those wolves are around and we are forced to attack them," I say. But Joachim is quick to remind us that we don't need to go through the doors.

"Our shovels and pickaxes are for something, people," he says. "We'll dig our way in."

And dig our way in we do. We count the blocks before starting, then dig down and forward. Past the wolves, beneath the hill, and once we're sure we're inside, we dig upward.

We come up into a lit room that looks like some sort of lounge area in the middle of the house. We quickly cover up the dirt.

"All right," says Aminata. "Now, we find where to hide. Let's split up and meet back here quickly."

We do as we're told. Soon, we're back, and Aminata has found a room she thinks is Declan's. We go in and see she's right: there are a bunch of armor items hanging from an armor stand. Next to them is something like a fireplace, with a collection of player heads—many of them very beautiful—hanging from the wall. From all the players he's managed to defeat, I suppose. I suspect he wears them every now and then, like some sort of a fearsome helmet. I wonder how it feels to put on one of those.

There is also a post nearby where a lead can be tied.

"Declan probably never lets the Talisman of Chance out of sight," says Joachim, pointing to the post. "Seems like that's where he ties him every night before he goes AFK."

"We hide in the walls, here," Aminata says. "Then we come out once Declan's gone AFK."

"Like silverfish," Joachim says. "I love it."

We go to work. Aminata ransacks a nearby chest and manages to find a few useful things, including some bread, baked potatoes, and salmon to feed to Cranky. She also snags a clock so we can keep track of time while waiting within the walls. The clock doesn't work right, because there's no daytime here. It seems to point in only one direction, which I think is the sunset we're currently in. By dark, I suspect, it'll point in the opposite direction, to night.

Joachim examines each wall, looking for which one has enough depth to hold all three of us without it being obvious someone's hiding there. I, on the other hand, have an idea or two. First, I ransack a few chests as well, until I manage to find three saddles—ordinarily hard to find, but clearly nothing is too hard for Declan and his gang. After this, I follow our dug path back outside and try to gather some leaves from a tree. I can't keep the leaves—they keep breaking—but I do get a sapling.

"What's that for?" Jo asks when I return, referring to the seedling.

"Nothing, actually," I say. "I'm trying to get leaves. We need to leave one block in the wall open so we can peep through. We can cover the opening with leaves. He'll think it's, like, moss or something. And then we can peek through to see what's happening. Do you two know the tool we need?"

"Shears, I think," says Aminata, looking deep in her own inventory, then producing one. "Ha! These will work. Good job, Cece." She hands them to me.

"I have another good idea. Come, let me show you something."

I lead them back down the dug path, and after pausing to shear off some leaves and stick them in my inventory, I direct our digging toward the horses.

"We may need to get out fast when we take Cranky," I say, once we reach there and have dug up to the surface. "So, I think we can saddle each horse now, and then take them when we're leaving. They'll get us around much faster and we can run from mob attacks and other players. We'll get back to the mountains in no time, and we can complete the Third Trial before you know it."

"Wish I could high-five you right now," Joachim says. "You're bursting with great ideas today!"

We each saddle one horse after I hand them the saddles from Declan's chest. Then we leave, return through our dug path, seal ourselves into the walls of the Iron Fortress, and lie in wait.

CHAPTER TWENTY-SIX

DECLAN'S RETURN IS NOISY.

When Therese used to join me after I'd get to Silver Oaks, she'd arrive with a *pop!* and I'd know she was around, and we'd try to find each other. In the same way, I can immediately tell how many Anarchians are in Declan's crew, him included, by the amount of *pops* I hear as they teleport into the fortress.

Six, I say to Aminata and Joachim, but with a direct-to-player chat, because who knows what devices these folks are playing on — they might hear us talking to one another.

Gotcha, says Joachim. *Now, we wait.*

I peer through the leaves, just to be sure. There is no one in the room out there yet. Just a jumble of chattering voices in the far background, along with sounds of movement, like when they step in grass or climb onto something they're not supposed to be climbing on. They have also come at night, which means there's a ton of zombies and the like out there right now. I can hear some of their groans. Maybe some crew members are keeping an eye out for anything more dangerous getting too close to the fortress.

And, just as I'm thinking this, in walks Declan, in his diamond suit and colorful patchwork head. In his hand is a lead, and at the end of the lead is Cranky, walking obediently by and purring.

I feel like my blood is boiling. This is the second time Declan's done this, and it takes every bit of willpower I have not to hack my way out of the wall and smack him over the head for treating our dear cat like this.

Easy, types Aminata, perhaps sensing my impatience. **Remember the plan.**

It does not get any easier to stay put, but stay put I do, waiting for Declan to go AFK.

I watch him tie Cranky's lead to a post, then throw some stuff in a chest—clearly stuff he and his crew have bullied some newcomer out of. He takes off his diamond armor and puts it in the chest as well. For a moment, it's almost as if he knows we are hiding in the walls, because he pauses, hand frozen, and then *looks* in our direction, at the very square with the grass.

He walks over to the opening with the leaves, where we're standing on the opposite side of the wall. All three of us—Aminata, Jo, and I—crouch and hold our breaths as much as we can. Declan has stopped just on the opposite side now, just a block away from us. One or two pickaxe hits, and we'd be standing face-to-face.

"Ooh, I must've done that," says another voice, someone else who has just come into the room. One of the crew members, perhaps. Declan turns away to speak to him, which I know because I can no longer see Declan's shadow over the opening with the leaves.

"I was trying to remove a torch once," the person is saying. "Maybe I mined the block that was there and just replaced it with one I had. Remember we went to the cave with all that moss recently?"

"Yeah, yeah, whatever," says Declan. "Just fix it."

The person seems to come close to the opening, just as close as Declan did, but then Declan stops him.

"Not *now!*" he says. "Tomorrow or something. I need to reset my spawn and I'll soon be going AFK. You people be on watch today. Hit me up if something happens."

With that, the other person trudges out of the room. I'm able to peep through the hole again, and a moment later, Declan has gone AFK. His avatar just stands there, unmoving, doing nothing.

Now, I say to Aminata and Jo.

Jo mines the blocks slowly and deliberately, hoping to minimize noise, and soon there is enough space for us to squeeze out through the wall. We don't wait to close the hole back up. Immediately, I creep over to where Cranky is tied to the post, only a step or two from where Declan is AFK.

Please don't make a noise, please don't make a noise, I think as I approach Cranky.

The cat turns around and sees me. I can immediately tell he's on his way to being Declan's, the recognition in his eyes almost all gone. He looks feral upon spotting me, as if he's gone wild in his time with Declan. As if I'm now the enemy. I have never seen Cranky look like this before.

Then he opens his mouth.

I'm all but sure, at this point, that he's about to swallow my weapon because I'm standing *this* close to Declan, his new owner. But I soon realize he's instead going to make one of his trademark *rawr* sounds, and that is *definitely* going to wake Declan up.

But from out of nowhere comes Aminata, a salmon in hand—one of those she's pulled from Declan's chest. She reaches forward with it, stopping Cranky halfway through whatever he was planning to do. His eyes bulge at the offer of free food.

Come on, I think. *Take it.*

And he does just that, swallowing the fish as Aminata lets it fall to him. As he gobbles it up, she passes one more salmon each to Joachim and me. I don't quite understand why, and I'm about to ask her when I realize there's no time.

I feed the fish to Cranky. He gobbles it up. Then Joachim gives him his as well, and Cranky chomps on it. Once he's done, a flurry of hearts appears over him, washing over me in the same way it did the very first time, when he became my own. But I realize that this time, it's not just one wave of hearts, but three. One wave for each of us.

He's now *our* Talisman of Chance, not just mine.

Now I see why Aminata gave us each a piece of fish. This is what she was betting on—that the Ocury did not necessarily think to place a limit on how many people could own the Talisman of Chance at once, especially if they bought his allegiance by feeding him together. And that bet has paid off. Now, Cranky is not just going to be protecting me alone, but all three of us.

We waste no time taking him off his lead. We creep back to our dug underground tunnel, with few sounds in the house but the sounds of the rest of the crew fighting zombies. I figure perhaps the rest are asleep.

Hold on, I write to Jo and Aminata, once we're at the entrance to the tunnel. **One last thing to do.**

I don't wait for a response before I creep away, back into Declan's room. He's still AFK, thankfully. I slink over to his chest, open it up, and take out his full-diamond suit of armor. I place my iron suit in my inventory, then put the diamond armor on. I also claim a diamond sword, a bow, well over a hundred unenchanted arrows, and a random collection of potions. After another moment of thought, I slip one of the collectible player heads off the wall and wear it as well. It doesn't feel as awkward as I thought it would. In fact, it feels nothing different from wearing a helmet, except I can actually wear my helmet over it, which I do.

That'll serve you right, Declan, I think, a parting shot as I slip away.

Back at the entryway to the tunnel, Aminata eyes my new suit and head. But she suddenly understands when I hand her the iron suit of armor.

Thanks, she types. Then she puts on the armor. I also hand her the new bow, as well as a bunch of arrows. Lastly, I give her my old iron sword.

We crawl back out through the tunnel, Cranky in tow. We follow the same pathway back to the horses, and once we get there, we mount them successfully, without stress.

As we ride off into the night, past the groans of gathering zombies too slow to catch us, I imagine Declan waking up to find his saddles, horses, suit of armor, and one of his collectible heads gone, and screaming his colorful patchwork head off. The image gives me so much joy that I find myself laughing, loud into the night, as if I am conqueror of Anarchia.

Once, I thought I was nothing, that I had no special skills to make people in this world or in the one outside like me. But today, I've learned that even the goofy, fun stuff I know and love can help me conquer hard challenges. Now, once my new friends and I complete the Third Trial, we will all be conquerors together.

PART FOUR

OLD ENDS,
NEW BEGINNINGS

CHAPTER TWENTY-SEVEN

"DOES ANYONE KNOW WHAT EXACTLY the Third Trial is?" asks Joachim.

We've been riding for an Anarchian day and a half now. We cut through Greenland quickly and were back into Desertland in no time, thanks to our trusty new horses. We don't even need our maps anymore, thanks to Aminata, who knows the location of the beacon that'll take us into the Third Trial. We're less than a day away from the mountains now.

"No idea," I say.

"Me neither," says Aminata. "I never got out of the first phase."

"The crowded-mob phase, right?" says Joachim. "I've been thinking. I think I know what the Third Trial is."

Aminata and I both look at him. "Oh?" we say, together.

"Yeah," he says. "Can you describe what happened the last time you put a Nether star in the beacon?"

"I didn't put the Nether star *into* a beacon," Aminata says. "There're five glass blocks, three obsidian blocks. You pick them up, and with a crafting table use them and your Nether star to create a beacon."

"And then?"

Aminata thinks for a moment. "And then you put the beacon on top of a netherite pyramid, which is already there. Once you do that, the beacon will activate, and the pyramid will open up a portal. You follow the portal and come out on the other side, and *wham*, mobs."

"The portal," asks Joachim. "What's it like?"

"Nothing fancy," says Aminata. "Kinda like the Soul Sand Valley one in the middle of the desert. It opens into the mountains, though I'm not sure that where we come out on the other side is mountains. At least, it doesn't feel like that. There's nothing there, just a large expanse of . . . nothing. The only place I remember is the room I appeared in, and that's only because it's where I got mobbed."

Joachim is silent again as we ride past a few spiders that shouldn't be out here in the wastelands but are. They hiss at us as we canter past, daring us to come at them. We don't bother—no point risking our one life each, Aminata and I, on petty things. Even the Anarchians we encountered, we just ignored. We have one goal, which we're so close to now. We might even make it before sunset is over.

"Were there torches?" Joachim asks.

"Sorry?"

"Torches," Joachim says. "Did you see torches? Or stone?"

Aminata thinks again. "Maybe? I think? I saw stairs, though. I remember running up them to get away, but instead there were just more mobs, reaching for me."

"And all around you, what was it like? Dark?"

"Yeah, definitely dark," she says. "Especially when I tried to run upstairs or something. That's why I thought it was inside the mountain, perhaps like a cave, but with a sort of room built into it, like we did with the Wither. But the beacon—it was there. I saw it, even though I didn't get to the top of the stairs. So I was confused—like, how can there be a beacon inside the mountain? It needs open sky to function, right? So it felt more like I was out-side instead of inside, but surrounded by . . . nothing. Like I was on the moon or something, and all around me was just . . . space. Like maybe I was on—"

"An island?" Joachim chips in.

"Yes, exactly! Like an island, but instead of water around us, just . . ."

"Darkness," Joachim completes. I feel the chuckle he doesn't let out when he says, "Oh, boy."

Aminata is standing stock-still, as if AFK. She, too, has just re-alized what she's not been paying attention to this whole time. She, too, has just figured out what the Third Trial is.

"What is it?" I ask. "Do you know what we're up against?"

"Yes," she said. "The Ender Dragon."

If you thought the Wither was our biggest problem, then wait until we meet the Ender Dragon.

That portal in the mountains that the beacon opens up to isn't just another place in Anarchia. It isn't even in this world! It's the central island in the place where Endermen come from: The End. And that central island is the home of the Ender Dragon.

From my last attempt, I now realize that the room the portal actually dropped me in is at the bottom of the central island. Which

*is weird, because there aren't supposed to be mobs in that room—
not from what I've seen in videos and heard from other players. But
yeah, I see how that's supposed to make it harder to get out of
there—if it's crowded with mobs, you don't even get to attempt the
Third Trial. Dead on arrival.*

*If we somehow manage to get through that—one or two or all
three of us—the Ender Dragon, the mother of all mobs, will be
waiting for us at the surface.*

"Whoo boy," says Joachim. "Now we're in for it."

We have arrived at the netherite pyramid, where the beacon
we must build will be placed. We dismount our horses quickly.
The mountains loom over us just like the first time. It's getting
dark, but it doesn't matter. If mobs spawn close by, we will be out
of here before they can do anything.

We get to work quickly. There is a chest next to the pyramid,
and true to what Aminata had said, it contains five glass blocks
and three of obsidian. Aminata takes them, brings out her crafting
table, and lays them all around. I drop the Nether star for her to
pick up, which she does. She lays it on her crafting table and,
poof, a beacon.

She picks up the glowing blue cube and climbs all the way to
the top of the netherite pyramid. Then she slots the beacon onto
the top.

The beacon activates with a deep, resonating sound, like a
spaceship starting up. It shoots light into the sky, humming with a
trilling sound, like a deep whale. And as soon as it starts doing
that, an opening like a black hole appears, and with it comes a
sound, like a beast's roar.

Shivers run down my spine.

"It's okay," says Joachim. "Nothing can come out of there."

But I'm not worried about what's coming *out*. I'm worried about what's waiting for us in there.

Aminata climbs down from the pyramid and stands before us all, cat included.

"We ready?" she asks.

"Yes," I say, but don't mean it at all.

Rawr, says Cranky.

"I am, but uh . . ." says Joachim. "Don't you think we should go in with some sort of plan?"

"Like?" asks Aminata. "Now that there're three of us—two of us with diamond armor—we can just beat our way out of that mob-filled room. Then we go up there and deal with the Ender Dragon."

"And you know how to fight an Ender Dragon?"

"Can't be that different from the Wither. We whack it till it's dead."

"No, no, no." Joachim is adamant. "That's a sure way to die. Listen . . . I may have a strategy."

"Better be a good one," Aminata says.

"It is . . . Listen," says Joachim. "Aminata, when you were in that room, it was filled with Endermen, right?"

"I guess . . . ?" Her tone isn't sure. "I think I was just out there trying to survive—I didn't really see much."

"But do you remember?"

"Yes, I guess so."

"Any other kinds of mobs?"

Aminata thinks for a moment. "Maybe not?"

"Whew," says Joachim. "That's easy, then! We don't even have to fight! We can simply walk our way out of that room."

Aminata and I both do a double take. "Ooooh! Of course!"

"Yeah," continues Joachim. "As we walk into that portal, we simply don't look up, and we'll never even have to fight them! We keep our eyes on the ground, and we can walk out of there and up to the surface, untouched."

Silence envelops us.

"That sounds *waaay* too easy," I say. "How can it be so easy?"

"The Ocury is sly, but definitely not slyer than us, haha," says Jo. "The Endermen are packed in that room because they expect you to be looking forward when you enter the portal. So when you land in the room—*wham!* Endermen everywhere, attacking you, causing you to look into the eyes of even more. No space for breath. But if you look down . . ."

I could see it now, and so could Aminata, her silence betraying her thinking.

"Seems like we can do this after all," I say to her.

"Yeah," she says, slowly. "Can't believe I didn't even think of it." She looks up, to Joachim. "Maybe *you* should become the Ocury instead."

"Nah, don't think it'll work," he says. "You earned the XP, so I think it'll go to you. Besides, you've earned it! Cece and I would never have come all this way without you. Plus, I can always be there to give you any good ideas I come up with. We're a team, remember?"

The beacon continues its humming, the portal calling to us. It's almost night now, almost time for every mob in Anarchia to come out.

"So, fighting an Ender Dragon," says Aminata. "Here's everything I know. The beacons around the Ender Dragon—not like this one; those ones are called End crystals. There are ten of them, each on top of an obsidian pillar, two protected by a cage.

And I hear the best way to defeat the Ender Dragon is to first destroy all ten of them."

"Yup, all *ten!*" Joachim sounds like he's seen a ghost. "And we also can't get too close to the Ender Dragon. It has different attacks—fireballs, dives, charges, Dragon's Breath. We can't hit it with arrows when it perches, only in the air."

"That's it," I say. "We're doomed."

"Not entirely," Aminata says. "We'll need the arrows for the End crystals. Also, there's three of us, right? We can have division of labor. We can do this."

I'm terrified, but the enthusiasm of my friends gives me some confidence, and more important, hope.

It's night. Hostile mobs are starting to spawn. I can see the sparkles of a few as they come to life not too far away from us.

"We have to go," Aminata says, then turns to Joachim. "Any last advice?"

"Remember to look down!" he says. "If we survive that room, we'll have done half the job."

We step into the portal, all eyes on the ground.

CHAPTER TWENTY-EIGHT

DON'T LOOK UP, DON'T LOOK up.

That's all I keep telling myself as the world about us collapses into nothingness, and then reappears. We're suddenly standing in a room. *The* room. The walls around us are green-gray, and the floor, to which my eyes are glued, is black. Obsidian.

The sound of the beast's roar, the same one as when the portal opened, fills the room. It feels like spiders marching up my spine.

"Nobody look up," says Aminata. I can almost hear the fear behind her words.

With our eyes on the ground, creatures start to move around us. Black limbs, long and thick and ghostly, circulate, moving around us, making *vwoop* sounds. Endermen.

I have never seen so many of them in one place before. They surround us so that we cannot even move our bodies an inch without bumping into one. Luckily, they barely move, either, not unless they have to. All we have to do is stand still.

"Nobody move," Aminata warns again. "Just . . . wait."

We wait. After a brief moment, Joachim asks: "Anyone see any other mobs?"

"No," I say. "Just Endermen. Jo, you were right." I almost look to Joachim, but remember at the last second not to look up.

"Okay," says Aminata. "Everyone hold on, while I find the exit."

Without moving out of her position, Aminata turns in a circle. The Endermen circle about her, as if sensing her presence, but unable to harm her unless she looks them in the eye. Aminata keeps her gaze down, turns around and around, until I can see her feet facing a particular direction.

"Here," she says. "Everyone watch my feet and face this same direction. The exit is this way."

We do as we are told, until we are all facing in that direction. Everyone except Cranky, of course, who simply circles us, *rawr*-ing as he pleases. Surprisingly, the Endermen ignore him.

"Move one block at a time," Aminata says. "I'm not sure how far the Ocury has modded this place—it's not even supposed to have an exit! But let's take it one step at a time so we don't run into any new surprises."

I follow the footsteps of Aminata's diamond boots, looking downward the whole way. Out of the side of my eye, I can see Joachim's iron shoes follow me as well, and Cranky's orange feet. We move this way one step, one block at a time. Soon, we're at the foot of the stairs, and begin to climb.

But there are more mobs at the foot of the stairs, as if waiting for us to come. They're all Endermen, like the ones in the room, but these are not as static, and roam the opening at the foot of the stairs. They could walk in any moment and come in eye-to-eye contact with us if we climb the stairs while they descend.

"Wait—hold," says Aminata. "Let's see where these ones will go."

We stand there, waiting to see if any will take the stairs, so we can refocus our gazes elsewhere. As we stand there, Aminata asks Joachim: "Any more tips in that brain of yours?"

"Not particularly," he says. "You?"

"Right," says Aminata. "Let's start with the resources, then. Everybody has good armor?"

"Yes," Jo and I chorus.

"Great. Who has a bow? Let's place it on your hotbar. Leave the arrows in your inventory, though."

I pull my bow out, place it on my hotbar. Aminata seems to have one and does the same, as does Joachim. I double-check mine for the arrows left from the fight with the Wither. Not very many.

"Now, sword. The more jacked up, the better."

The diamond sword I took from Declan's chest is already in my hotbar, so I just check that it's not worn out yet. Looks fresh, only a bit nicked. It should do.

An Enderman shuffles down the stairs, into the room. We halt all our actions and freeze, as it glides past us and downward.

"Okay, cooked food," Aminata continues. "If you have any, keep some of it handy. Fighting that beast is hard work. We'll need to quench our hunger from time to time." Then she looks in her inventory. "Shoot. I'm out."

"Here," Joachim says, and drops a few chops of cooked mutton. "Don't look up."

Aminata grabs it without looking up.

"All right, the last things we need are building blocks, any potions you still have, and a bucket of water."

"Huh?" I say. "That sounds bizzare."

"Water is to keep the Endermen away, in case we mistakenly look in their eyes when fighting," says Joachim. "There will be more of them at the surface."

"That's right," says Aminata. "And the building blocks are for climbing to the top of the pillars with the End crystals. And the potions are just . . . to make the fight easier for us."

We all ransack our inventories. Aminata and I still have a bunch of stone blocks from the dig at the mountain, some of which we share with Joachim. I don't have a bucket of water, but Joachim has two of them, and he hands Aminata and me one each. Aminata still has a Potion of Regeneration from one of the chests at our last hideout before the Wither fight, but she lost everything else when she died. I still have the Potion of Fire Resistance she gave me before we started out on the expedition, only because I kept it in a chest in our last hideout before facing the Wither. Other than that, the potions I have are two random ones: a Potion of Slow Falling, and a Strength potion. Joachim has none.

"Well, that'll do," Aminata says, then goes on to lay out the rest of the plan as we stand on the stairs and wait.

The three of us will need to do three different things. One of us will try to destroy the crystals, another to gain the dragon's attention and then run—a decoy, they will need to be very good at dodging and running! The third person will attempt to land ranged hits on the dragon whenever the opportunity opens up.

Aminata, who's the best archer among us, opts to go for the End crystals, so I drop most of the arrows I took from Declan's chest for her, and opt to use my sword if I exhaust the few arrows I have left. Joachim, who's much better at fighting than I am, decides to be the hitter. So I swap my diamond sword for his iron one, and also give him the Strength potion. Aminata drops the Potion of Regeneration for him, just in case, so I hand her the Potion of Fire Resistance, since the dragon will definitely be spitting at her once she starts taking out its crystals. As the last person left, I end up being the decoy, so I keep the Potion of Slow Falling, since I might be the one most often getting charged by the dragon.

At the end of all our exchanges, my hotbar reads:

- 1 iron sword
- 1 bow
- 22 arrows
- 1 Potion of Slow Falling
- 1 bucket of water
- 7 pieces of cooked mutton
- 64 blocks of andesite

"Okay," says Aminata. "Just remember the plan. Don't get too close, and don't shoot the Ender Dragon when it lands. When I'm done with those crystals, I'll join the fight." To me, she says: "Whenever you can, hide behind an Enderman, so that if the dragon charges you, it'll get the Enderman instead. Or even better, the Enderman will get angry and attack the dragon back!"

Once she's done speaking, I breathe a heavy sigh of . . . is it relief? No, I don't think I'll be relieved until we're done with this Third Trial.

"All right," announces Aminata. "To the surface, then."

CHAPTER TWENTY-NINE

THE SURFACE IS ALL VOID and nothingness.

As predicted, once we go through the opening at the top of the stairs, there is nothing but darkness and more Endermen on the central island at the surface. The beast's roar—which I now understand is the Ender Dragon's—sounds again. But this time, it comes with the flapping of wings, and a shadow from above, large enough to cover the three of us.

In the distance, the Ender Dragon circles around ten looming pillars of obsidian. It roars once again, striking even more fear in my heart.

"Remember," says Aminata as we edge forward slowly. "If you're swarmed by Endermen, pour some water. You take damage, you eat and get your health back up quick. Come on, folks, we can do this!"

We have arrived at the ten pillars. The Ender Dragon spots us in no time and roars mightily.

"Now!" screams Aminata, and we scramble over to our various spots.

I, the decoy, run headfirst into the dragon's line of vision, so it can see me clearly. I keep my gaze down so I don't stare at any of the tens of Endermen running around the circle of pillars. Out of the corner of my eye, I can see Aminata set up in a corner near one of the pillars and begin shooting up, toward the top of the pillars where all the crystals sparkle. Joachim, in some other far-away corner, quickly builds one or two walls of stone that he can hide behind and then charge the dragon when it lands.

"Yoo-hoo, Dragon-hoo," I say, trying to attract attention. "Come on, look at me, I'm right here!"

The dragon doesn't seem to be listening to me, instead turning its attention to Aminata because she has just taken out a crystal. So I remove my bow and shoot it. The arrow lands a hit from quite far out, which makes me feel giddy. So I shoot it multiple times.

It takes me a second to realize I'm only wasting my arrows, because the dragon simply heals again. Then I remember what Joachim said about its healing again and again until all ten End crystals are destroyed.

But one good thing to come out of the wastage of arrows is that the dragon has now turned its attention to me. I prepare to run. But instead of charging at me, it perches on a short pillar in the middle of the circle, faces me, and roars.

Out comes Joachim from his hiding place, racing toward the dragon, behind it and out of its line of sight. He jumps and lands up to five hits, then runs back to his hiding place as it turns around to face him.

I shoot two more arrows, just to keep its attention on me. They fall off its back and catch fire, causing no damage. But they turn its attention back to me, as intended, and it takes off and charges in my direction.

I must have miscalculated how quickly it moves or the distance between the dragon and me. One second, it was far away on the stone in the center; next second, it's right in front of me.

I have only a quick moment to remember to drink the Potion of Slow Falling, then it rears back its head and head-butts me.

I'm lifted up into the air, six or seven blocks high, then begin to fall, though very slowly, so that when I land, I don't take any damage. But while I was up there, I must have looked at a bunch of Endermen, because they're all waiting for me when I reach the ground.

At least two of them strike me before I can get out my bucket of water and pour it on the ground. That sends most of them away, since they cannot walk on water and have to teleport around it. I pull out my sword and finish them off. But while I'm doing so, the dragon spots me and shoots a fireball at me.

I don't dodge it quickly enough.

My health takes a small dip. I drink the Potion of Fire Resistance, hoping to stop my health from taking a bigger hit than it should. But for some reason, it doesn't work, and my health starts to drop even more sharply. That's when I notice a purplish fog, spreading from where the fireball lands. *Dragon's Breath!* I jump away as fast as I can.

Aminata has taken out five of the crystals. The dragon has circled around and is going for her, so Joachim jumps out and shoots at it, providing a distraction. The dragon momentarily forgets about Aminata, which gives her time to hit another crystal—six now!—and then start to climb one of the pillars.

I see now that the pillar she's climbing has a cage around its crystal that prevents her from just shooting it like she has the others. I see two such caged crystals. When she gets to the top, she hacks at the cage, and it breaks. Then she shoots the crystal from there, builds her way down, and heads for the second crystal.

Once Aminata has climbed the second pillar and broken the cage, the dragon suddenly appears out of nowhere, having circled back. We don't have time to warn her.

"Watch out!" Joachim and I scream together, but it's too late. The Ender Dragon sweeps at her with its wings. Aminata is knocked off the top of the pillar and, without slow-falling, drops rapidly.

Then, she does something really smart. She turns around and shoots an arrow as she falls, toward the crystal. It hits the crystal head-on, and the crystal explodes. Then she turns right back, just before she hits the ground, and drops two blocks to break her fall.

I can see the damage she takes as she hits the blocks, but I'm sure it's definitely not the same as a full fall to the ground. She seems okay, and gets ready to hit the next two crystals.

By now, the Ender Dragon has landed again and is getting ready to charge. I shoot it an arrow to let it know where I am.

"Hey," I say. "Look at me here!"

The dragon charges at me. This time I'm prepared, and duck clean out of its way. As it gets back in the air, I shoot two arrows at it. They both hit, and it takes damage. Then I shoot the remaining two arrows, and phase one of our fight is complete.

"Shoot at will!" Joachim announces, and for stage two of the fight, all three of us pull out our bows.

I'm not sure how many arrows we have or how many hits we land. I just know we shoot and shoot as the Ender Dragon circles and circles overhead. I also know it takes some heavy damage — over half its health, from the look of things. It lands again, and we scatter, reducing the possibility of the dragon charging all three of us at once. The Endermen, running helter-skelter around us, don't touch us, luckily.

The dragon chooses to charge Joachim this time, and he dodges well. It circles again, and breathes another mound of fire at Aminata, a huge chunk of which catches her. I see her quickly pull out her Potion of Regeneration and use it. Between that fall and the Dragon's Breath, it's a wonder she's still standing.

Then the dragon perches again, and Joachim runs out and begins whacking it from behind, dealing heavy damage. Even the dragon knows this, and begins to roar, then turns and charges Joachim. Its head-butt connects cleanly, and he's lifted up in the air. Like me, he doesn't have slow-falling, so he drops to the ground, *hard*.

Oh no!

I can feel the amount of damage he takes, and it makes sense he doesn't get up immediately, lying there with the wind—and health and life—knocked out of him.

"Get up, Joachim!" I say to him, but he's too far away, and there's no time to waste.

"Keep shooting!" Aminata insists, and I have to return to the main duty of killing this stubborn dragon. We resume with our bows, hitting the Ender Dragon with as many arrows as we can, dodging the fireballs it shoots at us. Soon, our arrows are gone.

Aminata and I come together, pull out our iron swords.

"From behind, when it perches," I say. "Just like Joachim did it." Then, just as the dragon lands, I charge forward, screaming: "For Haven!"

Aminata follows, screaming, "For the Ocury!"

We run out and *whack, whack, whack, whack,* dealing more

damage than ever, dropping the Ender Dragon's health to less than a quarter. *Only a few more hits now!*

The Ender Dragon turns around, as if preparing to charge us. We're too close to dodge, so instead of running, we just keep whacking. I brace for the impact, and so does Aminata. I remember that my Potion of Slow Falling has worn out, so I won't be so lucky as to escape a fall this time if the head-butt does lift me up.

Then, out of nowhere appears Joachim, running toward us, diamond sword held high. He screams: "For my friends!"

He whacks the Ender Dragon once, twice, thrice, just as we get our last whacks in. The damage is severe enough to take out every last bit of health it has left. It cries out in a deep, resounding voice.

Then the Ender Dragon begins to rise, slowly. Not flapping its wings, but *ascending*, like an angel. Beams of purple light stream out of its body, shining in all directions and piercing the nothingness with sharp illumination. Its wings and body begin to tatter as it rises, slowly, until it disappears into the dark nothing sky.

"Is that . . . ?" I can't get myself to say the words. "Did we . . . ?"

Third Trial Completed! my chatbox announces. **Congratulations!**

"We did it," Aminata says, relief in her voice. "Oh, we did it!"

Experience points and other resources begin to drop from the sky. Aminata rushes to pick them up, adding them to her own. When she reaches the amount she needs to become the Ocury, there is a burst of stars all around her, so bright they wipe out all the Endermen in sight.

"I got it," I can hear her say. "Haha! I can be the new Ocury!" She runs about the island, jumping and shouting a series of *whoops!*

Then—that sound again, the one of a new gateway portal forming. Just like the one that brought us here, another one opens. This time, though, it has a message at the top.

Welcome to Haven.

"Are you ready?" Joachim says. "To see your friend?"

I had almost completely forgotten about Therese. It strikes me now that though I might have started this journey because of her, I had seen it through to the end only because of the new friends I made along the way. Cat included.

"I already have my friends," I say when Aminata comes back to join us. "Haven is just the icing on the cake."

Together, we walk through the portal, and into a new world.

But when I come out on the other side, there is no one but me. I am all alone again.

CHAPTER THIRTY

THERE WERE TWO REASONS WHY Cece did not stay in Haven once the world had opened up before her.

First, because though the world before her was suddenly bright and airy and beautiful, all green and lush and flowery in a way she hadn't seen in a long time, it was empty. Not "*empty*" as in no people—she could see random players walking, running, chatting to one another, animals wandering about, with no hostiles anywhere. It was *empty* because Aminata and Joachim and Cranky were not there. And though she knew she would be seeing and speaking to Therese soon, her enthusiasm to reunite with her oldest friend had dwindled during the time it had taken her to complete the Trials. Now she only felt like all that work had been in vain, that if she could not keep the friends who had helped her complete it, then of what use was staying in Haven?

The second reason was that, as she stood there, taking it all in, Baba walked into the den IRL and asked for her to take off her headset and put down the controller. When she did, he was handing a phone over to her.

"It's your friend!" he was saying, his eyes shining with delight.

The good news was that someone from the estate had managed to speak to Mrs. Olumide from three streets down, and had mentioned that Mr. Alao was looking to get Mr. Njinga's new number from her. She'd given the person this information, and this person in turn had handed it to Cece's Baba. So Baba video-called his old friend and caught up with him for close to an hour, before remembering it was Cece who wanted to speak to Therese. So Mr. Njinga handed the phone to his daughter, while Baba handed his to Cece and left her to chat with Therese.

Phone in hand, Cece wondered how fate had it that getting to speak to Therese both game-side and IRL had coincided. Not that it was important. The reason she had been playing hard all this time now stood in front of her. But instead of feeling ecsatic, she felt only . . . *meh*.

"Hiii!" Therese said through the phone. She looked less dressed up than the last time. Her braids had been taken out, and her hair had been blow-dried and heat-stretched, and was now held up in temporary plaits, awaiting the next hairstyle. When she waved, she had a controller in her hand, like she, too, had been playing a game when her father had handed her the phone.

"Hey, Reesa," Cece replied, trying not to sound downbeat.

"Ohmygosh, Cece, how are you?" Therese rose and left for a more comfortable position. "So crazy that we've not been able to speak all this time!"

"Yeah, I know," said Cece. "So crazy."

"I feel so bad, everything happening like this," she said. "And it's all my father's fault. He didn't let me say goodbye to you—

didn't even let us plan, like, BFF last-day stuff or something before I left. And then we got here and it's been so hard to contact you and everything because we had to change phone numbers one million times, and the time zones are *eight hours apart!*" She sighed, frustrated, then quickly perked up. "But you made it to Haven! I just got the message over here."

"Yeah," Cece said.

"Aren't you excited!? Ooh, I can't wait for you to come over to where my bro Hashim's friends built a new base for me and them. Like, Silver Oaks is a shambles compared to this! But don't worry—you and I can still build our own thing, fresh and new. Haven has a place for everyone." She paused. "You're still on your old name tag, right?"

"Yes," said Cece. "But—"

"Ooh, cool," said Therese. She seemed to rise and pick up her controller, returning to her console and screen. "I can easily find you, no worries! These guys—my brother's friends, yeah?—they have some mad skills. They can find anyone they want with some cool commands and whatnot."

"Great, cool," said Cece. "Listen, Reesa—"

"I know, right!" Then she paused. "Wait. How did you complete the Trials?"

"That's the thing." Now it was Cece's turn to sigh. "I had help."

"Ooh, new friends, yay! Bring them right over, too. Just gimme their tags, I can find you all—"

"I'm not staying in Haven, Reesa."

It was out of her mouth before Cece could pull it back in. But there, she had said it.

Therese, surprisingly, did not look as upset as Cece had thought she would. Instead, she paused, thinking, then seemed to put away her controller again, and settled into a sitting position, her screen shaking as she balanced the phone on something so she could speak without holding it.

"Why?" was all Therese asked, when she had taken time to process it.

"My friends," Cece said. "They weren't allowed into Haven. And I don't think I want to stay if they're not here."

"Oh," said Therese. "Do you know why?"

Cece shrugged.

"Did they complete *all* the Trials?"

Now that Cece thought about it, Joachim had completed only the Second and Third Trials with them. He had not yet completed the First Trial: The Evoker. That had to be the reason he was kept out.

"But one of them had completed them all," said Cece, thinking of Aminata. "She had a huge amount of XP and was going to become the next Ocury."

"Oooh," said Therese. "So *that* was your group! Wow, congratulations, I didn't know you were with such a superstar! Well, there's your answer. The Ocury doesn't get to come into Haven."

Cece frowned. "They don't?"

"Oh no," said Therese. "It's, like, against the rules or something. They manage the servers as admin, but that's it. Or maybe they can come into Haven, I don't know. But we're not supposed to know who the Ocury is. They're supposed to remain anonymous to keep the game honest or whatever. Anyhoo, that's why your friend didn't get into Haven. They must've ascended to Ocury status."

"And the cat?"

"What cat?"

"Our cat, the Talisman of Chance."

"You can't bring the Talisman of Chance into Haven."

"Why not?"

"Because you don't need it. Nobody attacks you in Haven. It's the people of Anarchia who need something to protect them from others, and that's literally what the Talisman of Chance does. Bringing it into Haven ruins the whole idea, doesn't it?"

Cece ruminated on this for a moment. Okay, it was clear that she wasn't being cheated out of her due or something. But the fact still remained that she'd be stuck in Haven with random people she didn't know, save for Therese. Was that what she really wanted?

"I think I'd rather stay with them," Cece said, with a finality that surprised even her.

To her further surprise, Therese nodded. "I understand."

"You do?"

"Yeah." Therese wrapped her arms around her legs. "When we first moved here, I was sooo lonely! I missed everything— Gemshore, Silver Oaks, you. I would cry sometimes, just thinking about all the fun we had, and how I didn't get to say goodbye. Just from the time and distance separating us alone, I knew all our BFF dreams were gone. I desperately wanted to hang out with new people, people that were as cool as you and could make me feel as loved as you did."

Cece blinked. Her eyes felt watery.

"When Hashim's friends told me they played Minecraft, it was the only thing I could understand in this weird new place. So I just joined them. I quested with them all through the Trials— evoker, Wither, Ender Dragon. They helped me with everything I needed and got me into Haven. I liked the way it felt, that they cared for me like that. It reminded me of the way you and I always played—doing stuff together, caring for each other." Therese sighed. "So I understand why you don't want to leave the people who helped you like that, too. Because I don't want to leave Haven, either."

Cece blinked so that the tears forming in her eyes wouldn't fall out. She could see that Therese was doing the same.

"But I want to tell you that I'm sorry." Therese wiped her eyes with the back of her hand. "I focused so much on enjoying Haven that I forgot about you for a while. I forgot how you must be struggling, too, after we left so quickly. And I'm sorry for not thinking about that."

"I'm sorry, too," said Cece, wiping her eyes as well. "For destroying Silver Oaks."

"What?" Therese's eyes widened.

"What?" Cece realized she had just let her secret slip. "Er, right about that time—"

"You destroyed our base?"

"Not *destroyed* 'destroyed.' Just nicked it a bit. I was angry about how you left, how you quickly found new friends and everything. I hit the sign and some blocks, maybe?"

Silence burned between them. Then Therese broke it by bursting into laughter. She laughed long and hard, slapping her thigh. Cece had no choice but to join in. They laughed, doubling over, until they had tears in their eyes again.

"Whew!" said Therese at last. "Okay, that was fun. But yeah, don't worry about that. It's gone anyway. Plus, Silver Oaks was a ridiculous name anyway, right?"

"Yeah, kinda," Cece agreed. "Like, oaks are not silver. They're *brown!*"

"I know!" The two girls laughed again.

"So, what now?" Therese asked. "What will you do?"

Cece had not thought about that yet. She didn't know where she'd find Aminata or Joachim, or even Cranky. But there was no one else she wanted to play Minecraft with now, whatever form it took.

"I don't know yet," said Cece. "Find my friends, I guess."

There was a short silence, and then Therese asked, "But you and I—we're still friends, too, right?"

"Sure, definitely. As time will allow us."

"Yeah." Therese made a click at the back of her throat. "Hard to be BFFs from abroad and separated by eight hours."

"I know, right? But we could be other things. Pen pals, maybe?"

"Is that still a thing?"

"I dunno, not really? But we could make our own thing. Doesn't have to be in Haven."

"Yeah, I guess."

"Iya says friendships never really go away," said Cece. "She says we simply discover a new place for them. Maybe that's what this is. Maybe we need to discover a new place for . . . us."

Therese looked thoughtful, then nodded. "I think I like the sound of that."

CHAPTER THIRTY-ONE

MONDAY WAS A DIFFERENT KIND of school day for Cece. She did not go into the Gemshore Secondary compound wishing that Therese was there with her. She did not wish for them to go through first year of secondary school together, grow up together. Instead, she was just glad Therese was happy and fine, and that she was happy and fine, and that they had both made new friends. All was right with the world.

Or was it? She had yet to hear from either Aminata or Joachim, at least for her to tell them what she'd learned from Therese.

Half of that was rectified after morning assembly, when Joachim jogged up to her as she made her way to class.

"Hello, citizen of Haven," he greeted. They high-fived.

"Sorry you didn't get in," Cece said. "Therese and I chatted over the weekend. She said it was because you didn't complete the First Trial."

"Yeah, I figured," said Joachim. "I don't mind, though."

"You don't?"

"Yeah. I never went on the quest because of Haven or anything. I went because of you."

"Oh?"

"You seemed to *really* want to get there. I came along because I felt it'd make you happy if you got to Haven. We had just become friends, and I thought, *This is what friends do, right? Help each other, be there for each other.*"

Cece nodded. He was right. That was what friends indeed did.

"Well, I'm not staying," she said. "I'm going back to Anarchia if it means I can't hang out with you and Aminata anymore. I can't even take Cranky into Haven!"

"Yeah, he's with me," said Joachim. "He and I got held back. When I realized what was happening, I just took him back to our last hideout and waited there to see if either of you two would show up."

"Well, just keep yourselves there. I'll be coming back. Then we'll go find Her Excellency, Aminata the Ocury."

They laughed.

"It's boring without you two, though," he said. "I don't think I'd want to play without you two, either. Especially with Declan's crew still out there."

"Unless . . . the new Ocury does something about them." Cece massaged her chin. "We need to talk to Aminata soon."

The school day went by with minimal fuss. Cece realized that some of the subjects and topics she'd been struggling with weren't that bad, especially now that her mind was no longer occupied and was freed from the shackles of worry. She paid sincere attention and found that her performance in class improved considerably. Her parents would be proud. *She* was even prouder.

Later in the day, a teacher announced that a seat had opened up by the window, and that anyone who wanted it could have it. Cece surprised herself by standing up and claiming the seat. She moved her stuff over and sat next to the window, a completely odd feeling. She was officially a *windower* now. No more hiding.

Other things seemed to be looking up, too. During break, while she and Joachim hung out at their usual spot in the food court, Ofure came by and said *hi*. She was alone, without the group of friends who usually went around with her. Cece and Joachim returned the greeting. She was about to leave when Cece asked if she wanted to sit and chat with them for a bit? Ofure thought about it for a moment, then smiled. Actually *smiled*, something Cece had never seen her do before.

But she eventually declined. *Next time*, she said, and went to sit with another group of people. Cece counted it as a win, though.

But the day wasn't finished with its surprises. At the close of the school day, as Cece and Joachim sat in the waiting area of the car park, Joachim received a text message. It contained the coordinates to a location, as well as the following note:

You are invited to Haven 2.0. Come if you love fun. No need to traverse the land anew, for you are no longer bound by the rules of the old land called Anarchia. Come as you wish — fly, teleport, ride — but come all the same.

Signed: *Your dearest Ocury. x*

"It's Aminata!" Joachim announced, grinning, then paused. "Did you get one, too?"

"I don't have a phone, remember?" said Cece. "But don't worry—I'll check my console when I get home. She sometimes sends me messages there."

"If you don't find anything, let me know," he said. "I'll remind her to send you one!"

But when Cece got home and turned on her console in the den, there it was, the exact same message, with the exact same location coordinates. She wondered what exactly was in this *"Haven 2.0"* as she put on her headphones and picked up her controller. Hopefully, not more mobs. She was tired of mobs, and fighting, and conquering and questing. For now, all she wanted was just to hang out with her friends.

That was all that filled her mind as she slipped into the world of Minecraft, curious about what new reality awaited her.

This place is not familiar.

At first it looks like the desert wastelands, what with its undulating land and never-endingness. Eerily similar to the very place I was dropped when I first joined this game. But as I look at it more I realize that it's still the desert wastelands, except that they're not wastelands anymore. Instead, it's all green, with rolling hills and flowers and trees. And daylight! Pure, unadulterated, bright daylight. Just like I saw in Haven when I first joined in.

And then I spot him. A blot of orange bounding toward me, all happy and excited.

"Cranky!" I scream. I run over before realizing I can't quite pet him without some salmon. I reach into my inventory, only to find it . . . empty.

No armor, no resources, no weapons . . . nothing. Just like the very first day I landed in Anarchia. Interesting how so much has changed, yet so much is still so familiar.

Rawr, says Cranky.

"Well *that* hasn't changed," I say, laughing.

Joachim comes within sight. He is no longer in iron armor,

but is dressed in plain clothes. I look down at myself and realize my own armor has been traded for plain clothes, too. The only thing I have left from my journey to Haven is the colored head from Declan, which I'm still wearing.

"About time," says Joachim. "Come, Aminata is just over this hill."

We go over the hill, and I see Aminata peering into a collection of chests. A fresh lake shimmers in the sun a few blocks away from her, stretching forward to where land continues on the opposite side. I can see a couple of squids opening and closing, swimming like sponges with eyes. A wooden boat is docked at the edge of the lake. Cranky runs to peer into the water, longingly watching salmon and cod swim by.

Aminata looks up and sees us coming. She's dressed the exact same way I found her in the hideout after the Wither fight, her hair the same shocking blue.

"Welcome to Haven 2.0," she says, waving her arm around in a sweeping gesture. "What do you think?"

"Did you remove the *whole* desert?" I ask.

"No, just this small corner of the world," she says. "And hello to you, too."

"Sorry, sorry. I'm just amazed by everything. And happy to see you! I was so confused about where you went after we fought the dragon."

"Ascended into Ocury-hood, is what. I was basically removed from this world. But I then received control of all the servers, all the mods, everything. Didn't meet the old Ocury, though—just, *Here are the keys, now drive*. But that's cool. Now I can do whatever I want."

"For real?"

"For real. But I don't want to do *'whatever.'* I don't want to be selfish. I want to make this place what *everyone* wants it to be, not just me."

"How will you know what everyone wants?" Joachim asks.

"I won't," says Aminata. "Which is why I've called you here." She turns and faces the large expanse of grassland behind her. "From our base, here, we will make those decisions. Together."

"Base?" I ask.

"Yes," she says. "We will build a base here. I can generate it, but that would be *my* thing. So, instead, I want us to gather materials and build it together. We can also take whatever we want from these randomly generated chests. Don't worry, even I don't know what's in them."

"Sounds like fun," says Joachim. I'm sure if he could rub his hands together, he would.

"Definitely better than slaving to complete some Trial just to live a good life here," says Aminata. "That's why I reenabled teleporting for everyone, and even added flying. Sure, there's still day and night and there are still hostile mobs and whatnot, but you don't have to fight them if you don't want or need to. No more Trials. Everyone will be allowed to pet and feed Cranky if they want."

"And what of people like Declan and his crew?" Jo asks. "They're still out there, right? Their buddy the old Ocury is gone, but you know they'll still be angry we took all their stuff."

"True," says Aminata. "We'll face Declan, together, like we always have. If it comes to that at all. I'm hoping he'll have changed now that the world itself has changed. Maybe we'll never have to fight or argue again now that he doesn't have to worry about a fellow player attacking him. He is now free to get all the diamonds and collectibles that he wants. He'll just have to get them the old-fashioned way: searching, finding, mining."

Aminata looks back to the location she has marked for the base. "Once we're done with this base, everyone will be welcome here. Even Declan! They'll come and tell us what they'd like, and I'll add it. We'll also go out and learn more about everything and everywhere and use everything we learn to make this place even better. It's going to be paradise, but not just for us. For everyone."

"Why?" I ask.

"What?"

"Why paradise?"

Aminata is thoughtful for a moment, then says: "Because Minecraft is about fun, and I've done too much fighting for too long. Now I just want to hang out with my friends in a cool, beautiful world."

It's almost word for word what I want. It's like Silver Oaks all over again, but its own separate, unique thing. It's perfect.

"I'll help you," I say, and begin to open a chest. "First, we must make a map . . ."

The sun drops slowly over the horizon, and will give way soon to sunset, and then to night. And though the night may continue to be full of monsters, when morning comes, it will bring with it a brand-new day of laughter, fun, and friends in the brand-new paradise of Haven 2.0.

ACKNOWLEDGMENTS

My sincere thanks to the folks who made this possible: Eddie Schneider, my agent; Alex Davis, story-making partner-in-crime and this project's editor at Del Rey; Alex Wiltshire and the rest of the supporting team at Mojang. This book wouldn't exist without you folks.

Huge appreciation goes to family and friends who supported my decision to write this book mid-pandemic: my spouse, Dami, for the chuckles when I would announce, after many hours playing at the console, "But I'm only playing for research!"; my Slack group of Minecraft-playing friends, who agreed to run some scenarios with me; and my teenage brother, the first person I ever played Minecraft with.

Lastly, to my teenage self who, when playing this game, would become frustrated that nighttime—and the monsters with it—arrived too often.

ABOUT THE AUTHOR

Suyi Davies is a Nigerian author of fantasy and science fiction. He has written works for younger readers, the latest of which is *Minecraft: The Haven Trials*. He lives in the snowy city of Ottawa, Canada.

suyidavies.com
Twitter: @suyidavies
Instagram: @suyidavies

ABOUT THE TYPE

This book was set in Electra, a typeface designed for Linotype by W. A. Dwiggins, the renowned type designer (1880–1956). Electra is a fluid typeface, avoiding the contrasts of thick and thin strokes that are prevalent in most modern typefaces.